D0038637

A PERFECT CEMETERY

First published by Charco Press 2021
Charco Press Ltd., Office 59, 44-46 Morningside Road,
Edinburgh EH10 4BF

'Silvi and Her Dark Night' was first published under a different title and in an
earlier version by *Granta* (#113) and *Granta en Español* (#11).

Work published with funding from the 'Sur' Translation Support Programme
of the Ministry of Foreign Affairs of Argentina / Obra editada en el marco
del Programa 'Sur' de Apoyo a las Traducciones del Ministerio de Relaciones
Exteriores y Culto de la República Argentina.

ISBN: 9781916277861
e-book: 9781916277892

www.charcopress.com

Edited by Ellen Jones
Senior Editor Fionn Petch
Cover design by Pablo Font
Typeset by Laura Jones
Proofread by Fiona Mackintosh

2 4 6 8 10 9 7 5 3 1

Federico Falco

A PERFECT CEMETERY

Translated by
Jennifer Croft

For José Adamo

CONTENTS

THE HARES

The king of the hares finished his coffee, put out the
fire and set his cup down on a rock that was still hot.
Then he picked up the bones left over from last night
and headed up the hill.

Higher, the pine forest opened up onto a meadow
of overgrown weeds the wind had made scragglier. With
every step the king of the hares had to disentangle leaves
that were warped by the dew, his trousers getting soaked
through around the ankles, his boots getting coated in
a fine spew of flimsy straw and wisps. In the night a
mass of clouds had stalled over the mountaintop, and as
the king made his way up through the meadow, the air
around him got denser, a cold mist in almost invisible
gusts making him shiver.

Halfway there, the king of the hares found an owl
feather balanced on a shrub. He took it by its shaft and
held it up against the light, spinning it slowly: it was
perfect, brown with black bands, without so much as a
single little cleft in it. The king tucked the feather in his
satchel with the bones and then kept going.

The altar stood clear at the edge of the meadow, just
before you came to the top of the hill. It was a large flat
rock, host to a modest heap of offerings. Adornments of
honey locust pods and wildflowers, spines and scapulae
interwoven to create a pyramid. The sun had bleached

the older bones, to the point that they had splintered, but along the upper part, near the apex, the greasy fat of femurs glistened still, and ribs went on oozing, ever so slightly, as they dried.

The king of the hares bowed for just a moment before the pyramid, and then he groped in his satchel for the bones from his dinner, setting them delicately up towards the top of the pile. At the very top he situated the owl feather in the eye socket of a skull. Then he knelt, and so he remained for some time, in silence, his forehead pressed against the rock, the grey tip of his beard getting tangled in the grass.

The hares didn't take long. They arrived and lined up in a half-circle, ears pricked, the slits in their noses probing the air: all the hares from the meadow. At that moment the sun shot up over the mountain, a diagonal ray dyeing their coats orange.

When the king got back up, he found the leveret crouched before the pyramid. It quivered but kept very still, the fluttering of its heart at its neck as its eyes flitted around. The king took it by its ears and held it up to the others. The row of hares bowed their heads, in silence, and in three hops they had all vanished back into the meadow.

And then the king twirled the leveret around in the air, dislocating its vertebrae. He popped open his penknife and pressed its tip into the leveret's white fluff, searching for the vein. Blood poured out onto the rock and the tall blades of grass and the sprigs that sprawled over his path as the king of the hares went back towards the pine forest, walking slowly, carrying the baby hare by its back feet, face down. Its nose, suddenly run dry, dragged along the ground, its head drumming between the scrub and the verbena.

By the time he'd finished eating, the sun had removed the dew from the grass, and the king of the hares was able to lie down on his back and shut his eyes and let the bright light of morning put him to sleep. The leveret's hide was airing out next to the mouth of the cave, clean and taut, bisected twice by poplar twigs. Above, in the perfectly celestial sky, a buzzard circled, but very high above.

Once, a couple of years earlier, the king of the hares had killed a buzzard. He'd only had to fire his shotgun once and the beast had come hurtling down, heavy, flapping. The king of the hares had nailed it up then in the fork of a pine tree, facing the meadow, its wings apart, its guts spilling out of a gash down its belly. He left it there as a lesson to the other buzzards, and the harriers and the caracaras, until all that was left of it was just some desiccated feathers stuck to a carcass. Then, when summer came, a storm ripped off one of its wings, and the skeleton split in two and was from then on at the mercy of the wind, always on the verge of collapse. By that time the other buzzards only ever flew over, never visiting the meadow.

In the afternoon it clouded over again, and a dark storm overtook the peaks with its bilious blue belly. It thundered twice, there was a bolt of lightning, and the hares ran into their burrows and huddled in tight, piling on top of one another and waiting for it to clear. It rained and rained, and the king had to cover his shoulders with a nylon bag. The moisture puffed up the landscape and softened the pine branches, their bark getting porous and tender. Sitting in the mouth of the cave, the king of the hares nibbled on some grass. He had no way to make a fire or heat up water. In the fissure he used as a shelf he'd lined up his pack of candles, his plastic box of matches, his salt, his pills for tooth pain, a Bible in a plastic bag and a few tins of peaches. His shotgun rested up against the rock at the back. Even deeper, where the water didn't usually get, the king had piled up the hides he used as a bed.

It got dark and kept raining, a peaceful drizzle, but from time to time it picked up, became torrential. The king of the hares could hear it making its way in waves over the meadow, until the deluge breached the awning of branches and clattered against his nylon bag. Then, in the darkness, the softer rain returned.

The water seeped down through the rock, and later in the night the ceiling of the cave started to release big drops of it. And so it rained on the container of matches and the little aluminium stove and the hides and the tinned peaches, and the king swore under his breath and tried to cover everything with old plastic bags from the supermarket.

By dawn it was no longer raining. A skinny fox made its way into the grassy scrubland and stalked its paths. Cantering, its tail taut, it went from one end to the other, its nose gauging the ground, its ears erect. It paused a few times, retraced its steps, sniffing between the shrubs. The king watched it from his cave, shotgun in hand. The water slid off the fox's back, but its chest and its feet were covered in mud. When it found one of their burrows, the hares hopped up and ran. The fox bounded after them, its tail waving now, tossing water everywhere. The king sat the shotgun on his shoulder and got the fox in his sights. The shot felled the fox, blew back its body onto the grass. Shaken, the hares stopped where they were, off in the distance, and stood staring as, slowly but surely, their chests all calmed.

A little bit of wind picked up and parted the clouds as though layer by layer. At the mouth of the cave the last drops slid over the plastic. The king of the hares was drenched. His fingertips were no more than white wrinkles. As soon as the sun came out a little, the king undressed and hung his clothes on a rope between the trees. His bulky, smelly sweater, his socks, his undershirt, his trousers. He brought the pile of hides out from the cave and spread them out on the grass to dry. When he had finished, he sat down on a rock, held his breath and wrapped both his arms around himself and held on. He let his teeth chatter until they didn't. His hair was a cold curtain over his face, and it untacked in grizzled locks. After a while, the wind got round to drying off his back.

Early that evening the king of the hares dragged the fox by its tail to the edge of the meadow. He nailed it midway up the stump of a pine that a different storm had taken down with a bolt of lightning. For the next couple of days he went to look at it, watching its thorax swell up and its black tongue be covered in worms.

Over the summer, the lowlands under the peak grew thick with thistle, stiff, with leaves in crucifixes on either side of the stem. Wasps and bumblebees buzzed over them, and when the wind swayed them, their leaves grazed together and made a noise like paper being torn. On hot nights everything slowed, ecstatic. There was no bats' flapping, no owls' singing, and the hares never emerged from their warren. The king slept atop a bed of watercress, at the edge of the dry slope in a swamped hollow that smelled foetid but stayed cool. Here and there a sound from the town made it into the meadow: mostly barking dogs, but gusts of music, too, when there were weddings, and, on New Year's Eve, the thunder-flashes, then the dazzle of the fireworks.

Early in the morning the heat would wane, the crickets chirp. The pines would creak, relieved, stretching as the wood cracked up and down its veins, all along the length of them. Then the sun would rise, and the cicadas would buzz like saws. Things stilled as the air seemed to inflate. By noon the hares were thirsty, and the king would take his clothes off and lie down in the middle of the meadow. He'd close his eyes and let the sunshine penetrate his eyelids. White dots would form and squirm over his pupils and make S's in that rosy dark.

The king of the hares would breathe deeply, and the sun would send a golden ray to rest upon his forehead, undulating gently in his brain, licking the insides of his skull. The sunlight filled the cavity of his mouth, came down along his neck, took his shoulders, his arms, his hands. It came around his every vertebra, every bone, and made them glow and raised them. The king would stay this way, suspended, feeling the wisps of straw come unstuck from his back. The light parted him from the meadow, from the stems, from the crushed leaves. Then the king of the hares would rise, fingertips barely grazing the grass. Moisture would slide over his body, rivulets rushing down his temples, down his legs, down his back. Sweat would unspool onto the ground, and then the hares would slowly venture closer, crouching in among the flowers, sticking their heads out to lap up what they could.

Around the beginning of autumn the king ran out of matches. For a few days he kept the fire ongoing, tending to its embers. As soon as there was a moonless night with a clear sky, the king slung his satchel over his shoulder, tied his bootlaces tight and went down through the pine forest to the crossing, following a path that only he knew.

It took him nearly four hours to get to the old road. From there he kept going down, down and down, till he could glimpse the town at the bottom of the valley, obscure and dormant, nestled in the lap of the land. In the black of the night, the lanterns of the houses formed a network of pale dots that reproduced the curves of the river, climbed the hillsides and seemed to alight atop the mountains. The king watched for a while and waited for the last lights to go out. Then he continued on the sheep's path that zigzagged down the hill.

He took his shoes off when he came to the ford and hid his boots in the roots of a eucalyptus that a rise in the river had long since torn up. All around him the sound of the river on the rocks scattered in among the trees, and the sparse glimmers of the stars brought out only little gleams upon the water. The cold current encircled his ankles as he crossed. As he passed them, Turello's goats swirled together in their pen. The king was barefoot, and he took careful steps. In the darkness he could hear a goat releasing its urine at length.

The streets of the town were empty. There was only Camilito Jara's truck, resting peacefully under a carob tree, ready to start up again first thing and make deliveries. On the main street a drunk was lurching along on his bicycle. With every rotation of the pedal, the chain stay pulsed with a pop, and as the drunk zigzagged on into the distance, he murmured something, but his voice was so low it seemed directed inward. He never saw the king in his crouching place behind the tree.

Still sitting out in front of Betone's bar were two old guys leaning back in their chairs, their gazes adrift among the cypresses on the plaza. So as not to walk right by them, the king of the hares went around the block, treading in the shadows, flattening himself against the buildings. Finally, he ran across the street and entered the alley that skirted around the Electric Co-op. Old Smutt's dog recognized his gait and put his head out to catch mid-air the haunch of hare the king tossed him like always.

Beyond the vines that covered the fence, the king could see all the way inside of Wesner's house, the light on in the bedroom, the eldest daughter in her nightgown, spreading sheets over her bed. A hen clucked on a stick. The bases of the bottles in Calzolari's widow's rammed earth wall were gleaming. The king continued down the alley until he could smell the pungent urine of the bats from the abandoned pigeon loft. In just one leap he was over the earth wall and on the other side. Two streaks of his torch sufficed to remind him of this terrain. Nothing had changed in Baruk's yard. The king made his way between the boxes of sodas and old batteries and the twisted scraps of iron that had once belonged to a bicycle. All he had to do to get up through the louvre window was climb on top of one of the chairs from the patio and grab onto the window frame. He stood for a while on the rim of the seatless toilet until he could be certain that all inside was still and silent.

The light from the street seeped in through the windowpanes and cast the pantry into murky shadow. The only sound inside the shop was the refrigerator motor, a low purr. The king didn't even need to turn on his torch: he loaded up on matches, flour, salt, took a tin of chopped tomatoes, two bags of lentils. His secret so that Baruk wouldn't notice what was missing was to steal the minimum: if there were seven matchboxes, to only take one. Of the fifteen tins of peaches, to grab the two from the very back. From the box of aspirin, to remove a single tablet. A car passed by on the road and the king of the hares crouched down behind the counter, but the headlights didn't make it to the shelves, and soon the car was down the hill and gone. Before he left, the king took a fistful of sweets from a jar, three lollipops, one big bar of chocolate. Outside he was greeted by the chirp chirp of the crickets and the air drifting cool over the weeds on the patio. The king retraced his steps with his satchel heavy now, the town's dry leaves crunching under his bare feet.

As he passed by Biglia's house, he stopped to snap off a pair of roses that had climbed up over the little earth wall and were shining under the streetlight. The king of the hares was already picturing how nice they'd look the next day, posed among the bones, at the very top of the pyramid, when suddenly he heard a voice from behind him.

Who are you? What do you think you're doing? A torchlight fell on him.

The king raised his arm to cover his face. The light streaked across his beard.

What have you got there in that bag?

The king hesitated for a second. Then he scurried off.

Stop! Stay right where you are or I shoot! the king could hear the other man shouting.

The lights in some of the houses came on. All the dogs in the town started barking. The king ceased to be aware of where his feet were landing, and he injured himself on the kerb, on a piece of iron or tin. It was a mighty gash, deep. With every step he could feel the throbbing wound, and he kept slipping on his own blood. When he couldn't go on any longer, he hopped over an earth wall and hid among some plants.

The voices, meanwhile, were getting louder in the street.

Down here, this way, they were saying. A guy with a thick beard, down to here.

The king heard them racing up, heard their footsteps, heard people calling to one another.

It's OK, it's OK, he whispered to himself.

Please don't let them find me, he murmured with his eyes shut.

Over there, head for the plaza, the voices yelled, and then they seemed to fade away.

The king had landed at the Tánteras. The windows of the house were all shut, and no lights shone from inside, so they hadn't heard him entering their yard. Squatting, the king advanced between the lettuce beds and the tomato plants, bleeding. He tripped on something, fell onto the ground, heard a boom of bins. Old Tántera himself raised the blinds.

What's going on, Bautista? What's that noise? the king heard Doña Amanda ask.

Hush, said Tántera. Go get in the bathroom.

Hidden in the arrowroot, the king could see the glint of a shotgun pointing out the window.

I'll get you, said Tántara, and the shot that followed sounded all across the town and echoed up and down the mountain slopes.

Pigeons took off as though in a mass of applause, followed by the panicked clucking of a thousand hens. The few dogs that had stopped barking started up again now. Doña Amanda shouted from inside the bathroom. The king did what he could to run, dragging with him some bundles of wire.

That way! He went that way! the people in the plaza yelled.

Now in the town not a single light was still exting-
uished.

The king of the hares jumped over fences, over
rammed earth walls. Something scratched his legs,
something jammed into his hand. He got up onto the
shed of Broilo's funeral parlour. Leaving behind a trail of
blood, he made his way across it. A dog was barking up
a storm below, in outrage. The king of the hares climbed
up onto the roof of Visnovsky's carpenter's shop, his
steps echoing all along its tin sheets. The back part of the
storeroom gave onto the river. The king lowered himself
down by the drainpipe and hid his satchel in the grass.
Before leaping in, he tried to find the current's centre in
the reflections on the water's surface. His body sank into
the cold water, and he pulled his knees up, praying that
there weren't any rocks in this part. When he opened
his eyes, he couldn't see a thing. He was surrounded by
black bubbles, and it felt like they were caressing his face.
The murmur of the riverbed and the sand pressed against
his ears. In a whirlpool, all the air escaped his chest. The
king no longer knew which way was up or down. He
stretched out his arms, his legs gave him up to the rapids,
and the water pushed his body up again. The king of the
hares emerged into the dark night and gasped. The lights
of the town, smaller and smaller, behind him now. And
gradually the river calmed, and the king of the hares let
it sweep him along.

It took him three full days to get back to the
meadow. In order to avoid the town, he had to take a
big detour around the mountain, crossing pine forests,
barefoot, with his wound wrapped in a rag. When he
finally got there, he found the bones of his pyramid
strewn over the rock, and a buzzard picking at them.

He tried to frighten it away waving his arms, but the buzzard barely even looked at him and then went back to what it had been doing. So the king got his shotgun and blew the buzzard's head off. He had to spend all afternoon cleaning up the feathers and the blood, putting the pyramid back together. The hares watched him from afar. It took another two days before they entrusted another of their leverets to him.

Cristina arrived on the meadow one clear day around sundown. She came out of the woods like she was lost, walking with her arms crossed over her chest until she saw him sitting by the fire.

The king was whittling a poplar sprig. She was wearing a yellow dress he didn't recognise, carrying a crossbody bag, wearing her hair up under a floral handkerchief.

Oscar, is that you? she said.

The king nodded.

You've been here all this time.

I have.

Coming into town to steal food.

Once in a while, just for things I really needed.

Her hands flew to her face as she burst into tears.

The king of the hares kept his eyes on the ground until her breathing slowed back down. Cristina pulled the handkerchief off her head and wiped her eyes and then her lips with it. A cluster of hard grey strands were peeping out around her forehead, looking electrified.

Who brought you here? the king asked. Who showed you the way?

Buckio had told me ages ago that you were here, I just wouldn't believe it, said Cristina.

What changed, then?

What changed is they found your satchel. There were

even people who recognised you that night, people who came right out and said it was you.

What people?

Betone and the other guys from the bar. Betone was the one who started it.

Did you tell them it wasn't true?

I did, I told them over and over again there was no way it could have been you.

Where did you tell them I was?

Off, in the United States.

Doing what?

Working.

Did they believe you?

I think so, I'm not sure.

What about Buckio?

Buckio passed away, last winter.

The king nodded.

I thought it was strange, his house always closed up like that, said the king and went back to whittling his poplar sprig.

Did you come here alone? he asked.

Yes. I came up yesterday and the day before but couldn't find the clearing. I thought it was further down.

Nobody followed you?

No, said Cristina and opened up her bag. She took out some things and showed him. Tins of food, drink mix packets, some shampoo.

Did you bring any matches? the king asked her.

Just a lighter.

That's OK, he said. Come on, have a seat now. We'll get the fire going, there's some coffee left, I'll get you some.

Sure, Cristina said and came closer. The king of the hares noticed then that she was trembling. She dropped her bag on the ground and hesitated for a second, but then she hugged him, burying her face in his beard.

Why? she asked. Why would you just leave like that? What have you been doing here this whole time?

The king of the hares put an arm around her shoulders. He patted her back a bit.

Forgive me, he said.

It grew dark, and the king started digging around in the back of the cave, until he finally came across his old jacket.

Here, he said to Cristina. It gets fairly chilly here at night, we're pretty high up.

A leveret was roasting over the fire, pierced through by a little poplar wand. Cristina wrapped herself up in the jacket and sat watching it. The firelight blinded her to the stars, but it lit from below the pine branches and the gash in the rocks where the cave opened, and it moved in waves, casting the king's face in shadow.

Don't you miss the house? Cristina asked.

The king shrugged.

I'm settled here, he said, and he moved away to turn the leveret over the fire.

When it was ready, he gave her the part with the most meat on it. Cristina rummaged around between the bones a while but barely ate a thing, just a few little bites.

Are you cold? the king of the hares asked her.

No, she said.

Eat up, it's good.

I'm not hungry.

How are your classes going?

Oh, they're going fine.

Are you still teaching the older kids?

Fifth to seventh grade. María Marta teaches the others. Now this inspector woman wants to see if we can open a kindergarten, but they'd have to appoint a new teacher.

Is there anybody in the town? he asked.

Well, there's Kovach's girl, the one that wants to go and study education, but she can't seem to commit to it.

Which of the Kovach girls? The oldest?

Yeah.

The king said nothing.

Want any more meat? he said after a while.

No, she said. I'm good. Thank you.

When it was time for them to sleep, the king of the hares gathered up all of the hides and, kneeling on the floor of the cave, stacked them all up again, making sure they were as smooth and soft as possible.

They'll keep you nice and warm, he said.

What about you? she said.

I'll stay right here, by the fire.

No, said Cristina. Come with me, let's both sleep in there.

I'm filthy, said the king of the hares.

I don't care, she said, and she took his hand.

Once they were lying down, she reached out and rested her arm across his chest. A robust darkness had enveloped them, and the stagnant smell of dried sweat and wet animal. Cristina's fingers intertwined with his long beard. Slowly they moved downwards.

Tickles, Oscar stopped her, and Cristina pulled back her hand.

Almost right away, Oscar said, I'm sorry. I'm not used to that kind of thing anymore. I don't really care for it.

Cristina said nothing. In the distance, on the other side of the branch awning, the live embers crackled. Slowly but surely Oscar's breathing got heavier, and Cristina realized he had fallen asleep. She got up without making noise and, squatting, made her way out of the cave. She threw a couple more logs onto the fire and pulled the jacket in around her shoulders.

A swarm of buzzing insects was hovering around the column of smoke. Every so often one of them would hurtle down onto the flames.

Cristina stayed awake all night, and as soon as it started to get light she strolled around the edges of the king's encampment. She saw an axe resting up against the mouth of the cave, saw a little broom made out of ears of grain, saw the polished bark of the pine trunk where Oscar always rested his back. She meandered around the meadow, without purpose, letting the dew get her wet. When she made it to the other side, she came upon the pyramid of bones atop the flat rock and stayed a while before it, contemplating the acacia husks and little yellow flowers that adorned it.

When she turned around again, she found seven or eight hares peeking their heads out over the brownish scrub. Ears pricked, eyes vigilant. Cristina nodded to them. The hares didn't move. They stayed very still, behind their snatches of grass.

Back at his camp Oscar was making coffee. He offered her a cup.

Let me look at that foot, Cristina said.

It's fine. It's fully healed now.

I'd like to take a look at it, Cristina said, and slowly, she loosened the rags wrapped around it, until she came to the scabs on his skin.

You ought to get yourself a tetanus shot, she said after she'd inspected it. You're very skinny, she said as she bandaged him back up. And that beard, it doesn't look good on you, it makes you look much older. Let me trim it for you.

No, you don't need to do that.

It'll only take a minute, said Cristina as she rummaged around in her bag for her scissors.

No, seriously. I don't want it trimmed, Oscar said and got up and went down to where the slope was to wash out the cups.

It was midmorning already by then, and the sun had got up fairly high.

It's time you headed off, Oscar said. Otherwise you'll get caught by nightfall on the way.

OK, said Cristina, but she still took forever to tie her hair up and gather her things.

You can't keep going barefoot like that, she said once she'd finished getting ready. Where was it you left your boots?

Oscar told her about the fallen eucalyptus near the ford, the hollow in its roots, the rock he'd covered them up with.

Got it, said Cristina. And you'll be needing matches, disinfectant, bandages... Anything else?

Nothing else, that'd do me fine, said Oscar.

Do you have enough cartridges for the shotgun?

Yes, said the king of the hares. I've got plenty.

Just in case, though, said Cristina. In case somebody comes snooping around up here. And coffee, since you're almost out.

Coffee, you'll need me to bring you, Cristina repeated, before giving him a hug.

Then she started down the hill.

Hidden here and there around the meadow, the hares, from their distance, watched her go.

SILVI AND HER DARK NIGHT

1

On one of the last days of classes, just before the start of summer break, Alba Clara went by the school to pick up Silvi. She waited in the shade of a tree by the entrance, leaning on her bicycle, the black leather case pressed against her white blouse.

Where is it this time? said Silvi when she saw her.

In the Thirty-Three Houses. What do you have on under your uniform?

The dress with the flowers.

The pink one or the green one?

Silvi lifted up her hem.

Don't you think that one's too short?

No, Mum. It's barely above the knee.

OK, but tie your hair back. And those shoes are done for — it's high time we got you another pair.

I like these ones.

I've spoken to your father already, said Alba Clara. Tomorrow you're getting new shoes. Now let's get going before it gets any later, she said, and Silvi took the lock off her bike. The two of them pedalled slowly over the hot asphalt, heading for the mountains.

The neighbourhood of the Thirty-Three Houses lay along the main road, far from the town centre and far from the lake, in the area where the streets grew steeper and the town began to climb into the hills. They had some trouble finding the address. Alba Clara had written it down on a scrap of paper and, every three or four blocks, she'd read it aloud, as they went up and down the hills. In the end they had to ask at a little shop. It turned out to be one of the last houses, right up against the hillside. A young girl came to the door, holding a baby.

I'm his sister, she said as she showed them in. Half-sister. Same dad. I'm here because nobody else was willing.

The walls were holding onto the afternoon heat still, the windows draped in blankets. There was an oniony smell in the air, and the stench of heavy sweat, and cigarettes, and some metallic thing: bitter, maybe medicinal. The man was lying in a twin bed, facing a TV. His face was swollen, and his mouth drooped on one side. Below his eyelids, his eyes were two streaks of black gelatine.

Alba Clara unplugged the television and took the man's hand in hers.

What's his name? she asked.

Juan Carlos, but folks tend to call him Lencho, said his sister.

Lencho, can you hear me? asked Alba Clara.

The man did not respond. There were almanacs on the walls, naked women with their legs spread. Old almanacs, covered in dirt and cobwebs.

The doctor came a while ago, there's nothing more can be done for him, said the girl.

Alba Clara nodded.

Lencho, we're here to give you your last rites, she said in a voice that was firm but kind. It'll bring you peace and get you ready for your encounter with the Lord. Are you ready to receive the rites?

The man's gaze stayed fixed on the TV's blank screen. His hand hung limp in Alba Clara's.

I can't tell whether he hears us, said his sister.

How long has he been like this?

He was still talking yesterday, saying stuff, but he didn't know who I was.

Did he ask for communion? Did he repent of his sins? Not that I know of.

Did he make any arrangements?

I hadn't seen him in years.

Lencho? Juan Carlos? Can you hear me? Alba Clara asked again.

Then she signalled to Silvi to open up the leather case.

Capsule or straight to oil? asked Silvi.

Capsule, hand me the capsule, said Alba Clara.

The capsule was a silvertone pillbox where they kept the consecrated host, which Alba Clara now took between her thumb and her index finger, whispering something. She made one attempt, and then another, but the man did not open his mouth, and the host just ricocheted off of his purple lips.

Alba Clara tucked the host back inside the capsule.

Oil, she said, and Silvi handed her a jar with a big lid. Alba Clara unscrewed it, smeared some of the oil and ash paste onto her finger and painted a small cross on the man's forehead.

May the Holy Spirit descend and visit you, Juan Carlos, she said. May He deliver you from your sins, may he comfort you in your suffering and grant salvation to your soul. Amen.

Amen, whispered the sick man's sister.

Amen, said Silvi, standing next to the bed.

Alba Clara passed the jar back to her. Silvi put everything away inside the leather case.

Should you need anything at all, Alba Clara said to the man's sister. You know where to find me. Call me anytime.

I spoke to the church, said the man's sister. The priest told me he couldn't come.

He's getting on a bit, his health isn't good enough to be out and about at all hours – that's why he sends me, said Alba Clara. But you've nothing to worry about, I'm fully authorized. It counts just the same.

Yeah, said the girl. The baby slept in her arms.

How old is he? Silvi asked her.

A year and three months, said the girl as she showed them to the door.

Outside it was dark already. On the street a woman passed them on a scooter; a dog got up to bark at her. Along the mountain slope glowed so many fireflies. Down below, in the distance, the lights of the road along the coast glinted off the lakeside. Silvi bent her head and smelled her dress. The sick man's scent had got all into the fabric.

I won't be coming with you anymore, Mum, she said.

Alba Clara was removing the lock from her bicycle, and she looked at her daughter without understanding her words.

What now? she said.

It's just I can't come with you anymore, Silvi said. I've been giving it a lot of thought – all the time lately – and I've come to the conclusion that there is no God. I've become an atheist.

Alba Clara was silent.

Mum, do you understand what I'm saying? asked Silvi.

You can't decide whether to believe or not to believe in God. You're confused, said Alba Clara. These are not things you decide.

I don't care, that's how I feel, Silvi said. I've made my decision, and I won't discuss it further.

We're going to see Father Sampacho, right this instant, said Alba Clara.

There's no point, said Silvi. There's no use in you trying, Mum – I'm an atheist now.

When they got home, Helmut had already holed up in the garage with his airplanes. Yet again he had forgotten to turn on the lights in the yard or on the patio. Not even the lamp in the living room was on. One by one Alba Clara went and flipped each of the switches, and when the house was fully illuminated, she opened the garage door and peered inside.

Talk to your daughter, she said to Helmut. Her new thing now is saying she's an atheist.

Helmut sat up straighter. Candlelight illuminated his hands between the shavings and the little metal pieces of a landing gear.

What is it? he asked as he took off his glasses.

Talk to her, said Alba Clara and shoved Silvi inside the garage.

Helmut rubbed his eyes, yawned a few times and restored his glasses to their place over the tip of his nose.

Come and sit, he said as he leaned over to inspect a tiny notch in the middle of something that looked like a propeller.

Silvi stayed standing by the door, watching him.

Helmut would spend night after night like this, hunched over in his chair, winding motors, trying out a remote control, polishing – again and again – small wooden parts until the light of day would take him by surprise, creeping in at the window. Then he would hop in the shower and dart out the door so he wasn't late for work.

After a while he said, So you've become an atheist, as with his screwdriver he bore into one of the propeller's edges.

Silvi shrugged.

How's it going with that? she asked, gesturing vaguely towards the half-assembled plane on the table.

A week or two and it'll be ready, said Helmut. Would you want to come with me to take her for a spin?

Sure, said Silvi.

Your mother mentioned you needed some trainers.

The ones I have are fine.

Have you had dinner?

I'm not hungry.

You OK, kid?

Yes, said Silvi.

You know all you have to do is say the word.

I'm fine, Dad.

OK, OK. I'm glad to hear it, said Helmut. Now get on up to bed, it's late.

It's not late, Dad. It's not even nine.

Helmut lifted his head, sought the clock on the wall but didn't come across it.

Is it really? he said.

Yes, said Silvi and gave him a kiss on the cheek and left the garage.

She tiptoed down the hall. Alba Clara was in the kitchen, putting lids on pots and taking them back off. Silvi locked herself inside her room. She let her hair down, took off her trainers, her dress, unfastened her bra and took off her knickers. Again she sniffed the floral fabric: the smell was still there, strong, spicy, salty, and Silvi wadded up the dress and threw it into the pile of things that needed to be washed. Then she switched on the fan and let the breeze dishevel her hair. She looked at herself in the mirror. She looked at herself head-on and then in profile. With her hand she smoothed her fringe to the right and then to the left. She rested her chin in her palm. She looked back at herself in the mirror.

Alba Clara called in through the door.

Are you in there? she asked from the hallway.

What do you want? said Silvi.

You can't live a life without God, said Alba Clara. It's arrogant. Only an arrogant person believes in being able to do anything without God.

Go away, Mum! Silvi cried. Go away! Just leave me alone.

2

The first thing Alba Clara did the next day was go and talk to Father Sampacho. She found him in a corner of the sacristy, seated on a stool next to the wardrobe with the cassocks in it, trying to fix a wooden candlestick with wire: the base had cracked.

Father, what are you doing here? Alba Clara asked.

Father Sampacho started and looked up.

I was looking for the green chasuble, he said. Where is the green chasuble?

I have it at home, I took it because it needed cleaning. What do you need it for?

Father Sampucho shrugged, sighed and returned to his candlestick.

Father, I'm very worried, I have to speak with you about something, said Alba Clara and told him everything that had happened.

Yes, said Father Sampacho. She didn't come to mass on Sunday. I did find it odd.

She gave me this whole story about how she wasn't feeling well, she had this headache, said Alba Clara.

Yes, yes, said Father Sampacho, making a tsking

sound with his tongue. I've been expecting it for some time now, he said. I'd become aware of it. She's seemed changed – lost, somehow, odd...

She spends all her time locked in her room, she doesn't even make the bed, said Alba Clara.

It's her dark night, said Father Sampacho. Silvi's going through her dark night right now. That's what it is, he said and set aside the candlestick and hoisted himself back up with the aid of his cane.

Such a shame, such a shame, said Father Sampacho. Such a good girl, so faithful, set on such a good path. But when God wills it there isn't anything that we can do. Silvi will have to get through this on her own.

Alba Clara took his arm and helped him stand up straight.

You will need to pray, said Father Sampacho. You'll need to pray a lot, as much as possible, for God to be by your side through this.

Yes, Father, but I always pray, said Alba Clara.

It's her dark night, said Father Sampacho. She'll come through it. They always do. It's like the flu: it lasts what it lasts, and then it's gone. It's a trial God sometimes puts us through, but Silvi's good girl, she's going to come out of this stronger than ever. Still, tell her to come and see me. Tell her I'd like to see her.

She's not going to want to, Father, said Alba Clara. You don't know what she's been like.

Father Sampacho nodded. He'd reached the window, and now he stood still for a moment, looking out.

I suppose there's nothing to be done, he said. We must be patient.

3

School finished, and then it was Christmas, and then the town filled up with tourists. It had been weeks since it last rained, and the dry heat had become suffocating. The sun shone over the mountains and charred the roofs of the houses, the sidewalks, the crowns of the trees. From lunchtime till dusk there could be no question of going anywhere. Silvi would lounge in one of the easy chairs on the patio, keeping still, watching the street, waiting for things to cool off. Feeling the sweat on her body, the nest of moist down that grazed the nape of her neck, the pleather of the cushions that stuck to your legs. Sometimes she took a book out, but it was so hot it was impossible to read. She'd only flip through the pages, without actually paying attention, without retaining a single word.

Every once in a while a car would go by, or a dog, or a family of tourists going down towards the lake. One afternoon, Silvi saw two guys in button-down shirts and ties walking along the pavement, across the street. They were blond, tall, both in black leather shoes and full-length trousers.

Mormons! thought Silvi. How strange. Why would they come here? And in the summer.

The guys buzzed at Cirino's little flat, but nobody came to the door. They buzzed at Widower Krausser's big house, but he didn't hear them – at that time of day he'd be out on the yard, busy trimming the grass. One of the guys took refuge in the shade of a tree. The other rang the bell at the next place. Silvi could see, from her vantage point, Miss Angélica watching them from in between the curtains, then racing to the door to let them in.

Finally! Silvi said. Something interesting: Mormons at Miss Angélica's! And she went to the bathroom, washed her face and fixed her hair a little. She put on her check-print dress, made sure Alba Clara was still sleeping, picked up a cup and crossed the street.

She went in through the laundry room.

Miss Angélica? Miss Angélica? she called out.

Voices were audible, coming from the front part of the house. Miss Angélica came back into the kitchen.

Silvi, my dear, I have people over now. What is it you need?

Could you lend me a little sugar? said Silvi and held the cup up.

While Miss Angélica went to look in the pantry, Silvi crept in towards the living room. The Mormons were sitting on the armchairs facing the window. One of them was only so-so, his hair slicked back perfectly, pockmarks in his cheeks, big ears. But the other one was tall, with broad shoulders, beautiful, bearing a striking resemblance to a boy she and Alba Clara had gone to visit once in the hospital, the most handsome boy Silvi had ever seen. He had been a tourist, in intensive care because of a car accident. The Mormon had his same blue eyes, the same clear nose, the open forehead, the same pale skin – very pale skin – and a breath of golden down peeking out from the cuffs of his shirt.

Would you all like some coffee? Miss Angélica shouted from the kitchen.

The Mormons looked up and over to her. Silvi darted back behind the door.

Oh, no thank you, answered one of the Mormons, the one with the big ears. We don't drink coffee, our religion forbids it.

Some tea, then? Coca-Cola, Sprite? asked Miss Angélica as she pointed Silvi to the exit through the laundry room.

Time for you to go, she hissed.

I'm not going anywhere, said Silvi. I want to hear what they have to say, too.

No way, no ma'am. Your mum needs the sugar. Here it is, so take it to her.

A glass of Sprite would be good, one of the Mormons said from the living room.

Miss Angélica opened the refrigerator door, closed it, opened it again, put both hands to her head: she had run out of Sprite. She got her wallet out of the cupboard and took a note from it to hand to Silvi.

Thank goodness you're here, she said. Can you run over to Ferrato's and bring me a big bottle of Sprite? Get yourself whatever you want with what's left.

Such a shame, said Silvi, but that's one thing I can't do for you, and she put on an artificial smile. As you know, Miss Angélica, my mother never likes me going to Ferrato's. Even less so if I'm barefoot and in a dress as short as this one.

But the only one open at this hour is Ferrato! Miss Angélica complained. The supermarket won't open until five!

Silvi shrugged, arched her eyebrows.

Please, please, begged Miss Angélica.

Fine, I'll do it, if you let me go in and see them.

See who? The Mormons? But you're a Catholic, you'll get nothing out of it!

I'm not a Catholic anymore, said Silvi. I've recently become an atheist.

Well all the more so, then! As an atheist, what do you care what they have to say?

Alright, said Silvi, but then forget about the Sprite.

Fine, said Miss Angélica. But just a little while, OK? You introduce yourself, and you're gone. Don't even think about making yourself comfortable.

Silvi went to the stand and bought the Sprite. She placed the bill on the counter and asked to get her change in gum.

Tutti frutti or mint? Don Ferrato asked her, but Silvi was distracted, and she didn't hear his question, so Don Ferrato had to ask again.

The gum, you want tutti frutti or mint?

An assortment, said Silvi. Give me an assortment.

She couldn't stop thinking about the boy in the hospital. His dry lips, cracked, the plastic tube that gathered his saliva, the golden down, his eyelashes, his lowered lids. His parents pacing in front of the entrance to intensive care. His little siblings, in tank tops and flip-flops, sleeping in the hallway on a bench. For the three blocks back Silvi could concentrate on nothing but that. Then she went inside again, through the laundry room. In the living room, Miss Angélica was showing the Mormons photos from when she was young.

Back then I loved to read, Miss Angélica was saying, showing off her library.

Silvi whistled from the kitchen and held out the bottle.

Oh, good! Our refreshments have arrived at last. Two Sprites, coming right up!

This is Silvi, the neighbour's daughter, said Miss Angélica as she set out the glasses on a tray.

Silvi waved at them and smoothed her hair again. Before entering the house she'd pinched her cheeks to make them flush.

This is Elder Bob and Elder Steve, said Miss Angélica. Elder is the same as saying brother, the Mormons just prefer to do it this way.

Steve, Steve, Steve, chanted Silvi in her mind. The likeness was overwhelming. The same eye colour, the same facial features, long thin eyelashes, almost transparent, lids a little swollen, as though from dreamy drowsiness. Tiny blue veins that shone through the pale skin at the temples. And bursting out of him a bright and spicy fragrance: the scent of damp bark, of resin, the smell of mist and wood.

Come sit with us, join our conversation, suggested the other Mormon – the one whose name was Bob.

Sit over there, Miss Angélica said, pointing.

Scent of fog and grass, a green wood bonfire, tinkling of dew.

I'll just sit down here, said Silvi, sitting next to Steve, as close as she could get.

The Mormon whose name was Bob spread out some pamphlets on the table and explained to them how they believed in God, in Jesus and in the Bible, but in addition to this, since they were Mormons, they also believed in another book, a book that God had dictated to Joseph Smith, the first holy book written in America.

Silvi wasn't listening to him. She couldn't take her eyes off Steve's hands, Steve's fingernails, Steve's knees bent beneath the fabric of his trousers, his firm muscles, the taut grey seam. And his scent, his scent. That bright, fragrant aroma, the smell of moss, of stone in shade, of a crystal-clear stream.

As Bob talked, Steve unzipped his rucksack, taking out some books with blue covers and setting them next to the pamphlets.

This is the Book of Mormon, he told them. These copies are yours.

Silvi nodded and picked up the book. It was like a bible but thinner, its pages made of tissue paper.

How beautiful! What a lovely edition of it! The publisher must just be the best! Miss Angélica effervesced.

Steve had left his backpack open, and from where

she was sitting Silvi could see inside: a stack of other copies, a little Tupperware container and, resting atop it, a deodorant without a cap, an Axe Apollo.

Pine forest fragrance, getting all into Steve's skin.

Bob talked to them for almost a whole hour about the collapse of the Tower of Babel and how the tribes had come across the ocean, and about some gold tablets that God had entrusted to Joseph Smith for him to translate, and Miss Angélica spent this entire time nodding emphatically and saying how interesting, how very interesting, how perfectly explained.

We'll need for you to dedicate this week to considering all this and to consulting God, truly, sincere in your hearts, as to whether you ought to believe us or not, said Steve when Bob finally finished telling them the history of the Mormons in the New World.

If you ask Him faithfully, He will give you an answer, said Steve. Does that sound good to you?

Yes, yes, absolutely, Miss Angélica instantly replied.

Steve looked to Silvi.

And you? he asked her.

Yes, said Silvi and then lowered her eyes.

Steve smiled.

Yes to what? What does yes mean?

I don't know, said Silvi, and feeling herself blushing, she covered her face with her hair.

That same afternoon she went to the pharmacy and bought an Axe Apollo. She hid it among her winter sweaters, and each night, before going to bed, she'd brush it lightly against her sheets and on the pillow and the headboard, and then she'd put it on her wrists and legs. Then she would close her eyes. In the midst of this smell Steve would smile at her. Steve's pale fingers would caress her cheeks. Steve would hold her tight to him, seeking out her mouth with his lips, grasping her breasts in his hands. Silvi, Silvi, Silvi, Steve would say to her, revealing his armpit.

Come here, Silvi, he'd say. Come closer, lick me.

4

Saturday started with dark clouds amassed over the mountains, and the forecast on the radio was for thunderstorms with possible hail. As the morning continued the clouds gradually dispersed, leaving the sky bare. The temperature went up, and the heat got sticky, dense. Not a hint of wind, yet the widower Krausser decided he had to fumigate the rosebushes. He got the pump from the little shed, filled it with water and mixed the insecticide. He was about to start spraying when he suddenly felt faint and went back into the house.

I've got something here, like there's something stuck, he told the woman who was doing the cleaning, and he brought a hand to his chest and fell backward onto the walkway.

The woman ran across the street to call for Alba Clara.

He was mixing the toxins for the roses, it must have been that, she told her.

Alba Clara took Old Krausser's hand and tried to find a pulse in his wrist with her thumb.

It's not that, Alba Clara shook her head. Go over to my house and ask Silvi to bring the black leather case.

The woman went off and Alba Clara stayed there beside the widower with his mouth parted, his tongue poking out, his breathing like a whistle slowing down.

The woman took forever to return, finally

33

approaching on her own, clutching the case.

Where is my daughter? asked Alba Clara.

She said no thank you, she told me she told you she doesn't do this anymore.

Alba Clara nodded. Widower Krausser was unconscious, but all the same she gave him his last rites.

You didn't come, she said to Silvi later, as the ambulance was driving off without its sirens.

No, Silvi said.

He's been our neighbour all our lives. You loved him.

Silvi shrugged.

Leave me alone, Mum, I'm busy, she said, shutting the door.

That night, when she got up to get a glass of water, Silvi heard Alba Clara telling Helmut what had happened. She could see her from the end of the hallway: Alba Clara had her arms crossed over her chest and was leaning her shoulder against the entrance to the garage, the scant light of Helmut's lamp making her visible.

I miss her, Alba Clara was saying. I don't feel right going alone. I never know where I've put the case, I don't have anyone to hand me things. The other day I almost dropped the capsule. Yesterday I accidentally left the oil open. Father Sampucho says this will pass, that it's just a phase, but I miss her something awful, you can't even imagine. How strange it is to turn around and not have her right there!

5

Did you do the reading? Did you ask Him truly? Miss Angélica wanted to know the following Wednesday, no sooner had she opened the door. Her copy of The Book of Mormon lay at the ready beside the tray, the glasses upside down, the bottle of Sprite submerged in a cooler.

What were we supposed to ask? said Silvi.

Whether to believe them or not.

Oh, of course. Can I open the Sprite?

Do whatever you want, said Miss Angélica and ran the curtain back ever so slightly. For an instant the glare from the street streaked white down the side of the bookshelf.

Here they come, here they come, Miss Angélica said then and went off to get the ice and a little dish with cubes of cheese.

As soon as Steve entered the house Silvi could smell his Axe Apollo. He was exactly as she remembered, his shirt perfectly ironed, his tie with the tiny check print. Right away he took his seat on the big couch, and Silvi went to sit down next to him. Bob, meanwhile, took a video cassette out of his rucksack, announcing that for today he'd brought a film.

It tells of God's first contact with Joseph Smith, the founder of our Church, he said. It would be very useful for us to watch.

Oh my, but it's been years since I last used the VCR! said Miss Angélica. I don't even recall now how the cables all hooked up. OK, let's see, where are the batteries for the remote control?

Bob went over to help her and Silvi was left alone on the couch, with Steve sitting beside her. Silvi didn't know what to do and looked straight ahead, remaining still. Steve made a tsking sound and slapped his knees, twice.

Did you think about what we were saying last time? he finally asked.

So much, said Silvi.

And what did you decide?

Silvi shrugged.

I came back, didn't I? she said.

Steve smiled and looked her in the eye. It was just an instant, but Silvi felt his celestial clarity permeate her entirely, felt him see all the way inside her. Steve seemed shaken then, and he lowered his gaze.

How old are you? he asked.

Sixteen, said Silvi. I just finished Year 11.

You're very mature for your age, said Steve.

Yeah, I know, everybody says that.

Steve nodded and didn't say anything else. There was an image on the TV screen, but it was out of focus, with lots of static. Crouching down in front of it, Bob was saying there was an issue with the tracking. Miss Angélica was trying to convince him that they needed to clean the VCR heads.

What about you? How old are you? whispered Silvi.

Me? said Steve. I'm twenty.

Bob finally got the video to work, and Miss Angélica scurried to close the blinds completely, so that no light could get in from out front. A man came on TV, by a lakeshore, saying that over the course of many years God had sent many prophets down to earth, that Jesus had been just one of them, maybe the best known, but that there had also been lots of others.

Today we are going to talk about Joseph Smith, the founder of the Church of Jesus Christ of Latter Day Saints, said the man on the video.

In the darkness of the living room Silvi relished the heat from Steve's body only centimetres away from her own. Enveloped in his rugged fragrance, Steve's leg on the sofa, right on the verge of touching her leg. Silvi leaned back and rested her neck against the back of the couch. As though out of distraction, Silvi tilted her whole body slightly until her knee grazed the fabric of Steve's trousers. An explosion of electricity then, and it advanced in waves over Silvi's skin, but Steve said nothing: he didn't move away or move at all – might he not have even noticed? Silvi looked at Steve out of the corner of her eye, without moving her head. He was very still, sitting up very straight, staring at the screen. Silvi's heart was a lump of live coal sizzling under a blanket about to catch fire. It was burning in the precise location where her skin was resting on that rough hot fabric. Silvi would have loved to lie back against Steve's chest, rest her ear against his heart, let him hold her, caress her hair. On the screen, the host was discussing the pioneers crossing the deserts of the Midwest and Silvi moved her arm a little, stretched out her fingers, her little finger sounding out the air. The seam of Steve's trousers was close, so close. Silvi was on the brink of touching it when the doorbell rang.

Alba Clara didn't wait for them to answer. She opened the door and the white light from outside blinded the room.

What is happening? Miss Angélica howled.

Alba Clara seized Silvi by the wrist.

You are coming with me, now, she said, and in one fell swoop she'd yanked her daughter off the couch.

Steve uncrossed his arms, leaped backward, a mixture of fear and surprise in his eyes.

I don't want you going near those people ever again, said Alba Clara as she dragged Silvi down the pavement.

Miss Angélica was watching them from the doorway. Steve had stayed inside.

And to hear about it from the neighbours! Alba Clara was muttering under her breath.

Silvi lagged behind her, stumbling over the concrete, her mother's hand like a talon digging into her arm.

They got home and Alba Clara slammed the door shut.

I won't have you turning pagan! she cried.

I can let you get away with many things, but that I'll never permit, she said.

Helmut appeared in the hallway and asked what all the shouting was about.

Nothing, said Silvi, squeezing her wrist.

It was about your daughter, who wishes to become a Mormon! said Alba Clara.

I was just listening to what they had to say, said Silvi. I'm an atheist, so I'm not that interested.

Alba Clara shook her head.

I know they gave you a book, you've got it in your room. You lock yourself inside your room to read it! You spend hours in there! she said. You want to be a Mormon, don't even try to tell me otherwise.

No, said Silvi.

Well what were you doing there, then?

I have a crush on one of the Mormons, is what, said Silvi.

You have a crush? On a Mormon? You what?

Mum, Silvi said. I'm in love!

I'm in love, Mum, Silvi repeated. Do you not know what that is?

They've brainwashed you, said Alba Clara and covered her face with her hands and burst into tears.

They've brainwashed you, she said between sobs.

I'm so sick of you, Silvi said, and she ran to her room.

I'd better not see you going across to Angélica's house again, Silvi heard Alba Clara screaming at her just before she buried her head in the pillow and breathed in deep until the scent of pine forest filled her completely.

6

Silvi checked out a book about Mormons from the library and spent whole days lying in bed reading it from cover to cover, making notes, underlining ideas, copying out sentences into a notebook. In the afternoons, as soon as she heard Alba Clara heading out to do her sick rounds, Silvi would grab her bicycle and roam the town. She'd go up into the more elevated neighbourhoods, scour the cabana complexes, the rental homes, the area with the pools. In the town centre, the main street had turned into a river of people, awash with tourists clambering to get a good look at the storefronts. Silvi would stand up on her tiptoes on her pedals and try to spot white shirts and blond heads in among these throngs.

She would ask the people manning the kiosks, the guys who ran the parking lots, the cleaning women just leaving the hotels. I'm looking for some Mormons, she would tell them. Two of them, young men, both of them have black rucksacks. She would describe them in lavish detail, then, their hair, their hands, their ears. Most people had no memory of them. Some, just a few, would say they had seen them, a little while ago, Mormons, walking down the pavement – but where? When exactly? With so much work to do and all these tourists in town, no one could say for sure.

That's OK, they can't have gone very far, Silvi would say and get back up on her bicycle and pedal up the street and down the street, towards the lake and away again, until the shadows loomed larger and larger across the pavement and the old folks took out their chairs and sat down next to the trees along the pavement, waiting for the cool.

Hey, Silvi! How's it going, Silvi? they'd greet her with a wave whenever Silvi passed by.

Where are you headed in such a rush, Silvi? Who is it this time? Somebody on their deathbed? they would ask.

No, no, Silvi would shout. Unrelated matters. Nothing wrong this time! she'd say and keep on pedalling.

When she got back home she'd find Alba Clara murmuring over her rosary, sitting at the kitchen table.

It's for you, for you, Alba Clara would tell her. I'm praying for you. Wait a minute, I'm almost done, I'm about to get to the last mystery.

Sure, Silvi would say and walk into her room and shut the door.

A man mowing a lawn in an empty plot near the fire station finally put her on the right track.

I've seen them, he said. They're living back behind the hardware store. They rented a flat there.

And Silvi was off, pedalling at maximum velocity, up the slope. In lavish detail she described them to the man in the hardware store. She mentioned Bob and his big ears, his pockmarked cheeks. She told him of Steve's watery blue eyes, of his translucent skin, his golden down.

Yes, said the man in the hardware store. They're living here, out back, in a little flat. They're good guys.

Then he told her that they normally left at nine in the morning and that it wasn't until seven or so in the evening that they would return.

And then at that point they stay put. They go to bed early, you wouldn't really catch them up past ten.

The next day, Silvi went to wait for them. She leaned her bike against the entrance to the hardware store and sat down on the kerb.

I need to speak to you, she told them when she heard

their voices in the alley.

Does your mum know you're here? Bob asked.

Steve, one step behind him, looked down.

No, she doesn't know, said Silvi.

Go and tell her, and as soon as she gives her consent we can go and visit you at your place and have a nice long chat.

She won't consent, said Silvi.

Then you'll just have to respect her wishes, you're not of age.

I want to become a Mormon, said Silvi.

Bob let out a tired sigh.

Really? he asked her.

Really, said Silvi, earnest as she could.

Then all the more so, let us talk it over with your mum.

No, Silvi said. Not my mum, she said and got back on her bicycle and pedalled until her legs hurt. Then she shut herself in her room, held the pillow tight to her chest and buried her sobs in the fragrance of the Axe Apollo while imagining Steve without his clothes on sitting next to her. Steve rubbing her back, unhooking her bra, showering her back with kisses.

7

Irma Bustelo's in a terrible state, said Alba Clara that night, when dinnertime came. A tumour. In her brain. It spread immediately, it's taken over her whole brain.

Helmut nodded and kept eating.

I took her the sacraments, and Father Sampacho and I have already put together a prayer chain. It's not going to be easy to replace Irma, she's one of our best catechists, said Alba Clara, pointing to Silvi with her fork. Her son is your age, he went to school with you.

Yeah, Danilo, said Silvi. We started out in the same class, but he got held back, and then he ended up dropping out.

I ran into him this afternoon at the clinic, he's a good boy, very helpful, said Alba Clara. He got a job for the summer at the Fishermen's Club, working the buffet, he says he likes it, that he's earning good money.

Helmut turned a page of the aeroplane magazine he had lying on the tablecloth, next to his plate.

Maybe you want to go and see him? asked Alba Clara. Talk a little while, get him out of the clinic for a bit.

Who? said Silvi.

Irma's boy.

No thanks, said Silvi.

He seems like such a sweet boy. Maybe you could even invite him over for a snack one afternoon, or just take a walk with him. He needs someone to keep him company, even if it's just out of charity.

Not interested, Mum. Thanks.

Alba Clara squeezed her hands into fists, closing her eyes briefly, counting to three.

I know you're still going to see that Mormon, she said. People from the church have seen you. I heard it from Angélica, as well. You're running around like crazy, on the streets at all hours, on your bike, going all over the place.

So? said Silvi. What do you care? I don't get what the problem is. Is it his religion that's the problem? You'd rather I sleep with Danilo Bustello just because he's the son of a catechist?

Silvi! said Helmut.

I forbid you to see him again! cried Alba Clara. As

your mother I forbid you to meet with that Mormon.

I hate you! cried Silvi and slammed her hand onto the table. I hate you! I hate you! I hate you!

Silvi, have some respect, don't talk to your mother like that, said Helmut, but Silvi didn't even hear him. She was already on her bicycle, frenzied, pedalling.

She awaited them close to the hardware store, early – very early – in the morning, and then she followed them, keeping her distance, crouching between the desiccated flowers in people's gardens, hiding behind posters and trees, on her knees beside parked cars. She saw them ringing doorbells, going inside houses, visiting families who received them open-armed. She saw them being yelled at, having doors slammed in their faces. Bob was always the leader. He would establish their route, smile and introduce himself and Steve, and he would initiate the conversations. Steve would follow, a step behind, listening, taking pamphlets out of his backpack, handing Bob the copies of the Book of Mormon. Silvi saw them having lunch with white plastic forks, each eating out of his Tupperware, both seated on a bench by the lake. She saw them going to the grocery store, where they'd buy eggs, shampoo, white bread, some hamburgers. She saw them getting home again, and she saw that it was never more than an hour before they turned off the lights. Then Silvi would go back to her house, turn the fan on, spritz herself with Axe, lie down on the bed and imagine what life would be like with Steve by her side. Steve sleeping next to her, the moonlight coating his chest in silver. Steve making them breakfast, bare-chested, wearing only light blue pyjama trousers with white stripes, the fabric of them thin. Steve taking her out on a stroll, in some far-off location, some other location, that also had mountains and a light blue sky, but where everything was green, very green, and grass grew on the hillsides and there were rivers and streams and forests that grew tall. Steve unfurling a gingham cloth out over the lawn, a picnic basket, strawberries in a bowl, white wine, a clear little waterfall over the rocks. She and Steve lying down on their backs watching the tops of the trees as they swayed, slowly. Steve making love to her, the two of them naked among the ferns. The moist moss that grows in the shadows, Steve moving in waves, fleshy flowers, petals, long strands of seaweed like hair, undulating in the stream.

I love you, Silvi, Steve would murmur to her with his eyes closed. I love you. I love you. I love you.

8

Until one afternoon Bob turned around in the middle of the pavement as they were walking down a street without trees, during the siesta hour, and pointed his finger at Silvi.

We know you're there, he said. You've been following us around for days.

Silvi kept very still, crouched behind a stand with a flowerpot on it.

We've seen you, Bob said again. Come on out. There's no need for you to hide.

Hey guys! said Silvi. What a coincidence, I was just walking by, and she smoothed her hair.

Things can't go on like this, said Bob. Can we really not go to your house?

Absolutely not, said Silvi.

What about if we meet at Miss Angélica's house?

No.

Well, then, I don't see what options we have, said Bob. You have to stop stalking us.

Please, there has to be a way, said Silvi.

But maybe… said Steve, who until this moment had remained silent. But maybe we can meet in some neutral place, Steve said, and he raised his head and looked at Silvi.

Let's have lunch! said Silvi. Let me take you out to lunch! We can go and have some real food, with chairs, tablecloth, utensils. On me!

It'd be a bit out of the ordinary, said Steve. But she's been making such an effort, and showing such an interest. What do you think, Bob? Maybe we can make an exception.

Bob sighed. He cracked his fingers, ran his hand through his hair, scratched behind one ear.

Have you been reading the Book? he asked.

Of course, said Silvi.

Every night?

Haven't skipped a single one.

Fine, said Bob. A neutral place. But no lunch.

Then a dinner, said Silvi. I'll pay for it, we can go to a nice place, one of the restaurants in the city centre.

Absolutely not, Bob said. We never eat out.

What about breakfast? said Silvi. What would you say to breakfast?

Maybe, Bob said.

Please, please, please.

Fine, but no coffee.

Of course, of course, said Silvi, no coffee, no tea, no alcohol, I'll come by to pick you up tomorrow, at seven. Sharp.

Not tomorrow, Bob said. Next week. Next Wednesday. Seven-thirty.

9

There was only one place that served the kind of breakfast Steve deserved: the Lakefront Hotel.

Silvi rested her bicycle against one of the columns out front and asked to speak with the manager. While she waited, she peeked inside the dining room. Most of the tables were empty. In the background, out the big window, you could see the sun setting over the water. There was one cloud splitting the sky in two, rising in soft swirls, the sun dyeing the spirals orange. On each table there was a centrepiece, with flowers.

Are those real, or are they plastic? Silvi asked the manager once she'd come out.

They're real. Of course.

And for a set price you can eat however much you like?

You can go up to the buffet as many times as you like.

Is it the same food they have in the United States?

Yes, ma'am, it's an American breakfast. It includes sausage and scrambled eggs.

Silvi pictured Steve sitting by the big window, looking out at the lake and slowly chewing slices of bacon, yogurt with granola, pancakes drenched in maple syrup. She pictured him smiling gratefully, Silvi having returned to him the flavours of his distant homeland. Thank you, Steve would say to her. Thank you, Silvi, thank you.

Deal, said Silvi and reserved a table. It was pricey, but it would be worth it.

Then she rode over to the accounting office where Helmut worked, greeted the secretary with a kiss and asked to speak with him.

Dad, I need to get those new shoes after all, she said.

How much are they? asked Helmut.

Silvi gave an exact amount.

Helmut opened a drawer, poked around in a little box, grabbed some bills and gave them to her.

10

The night before the breakfast, Silvi barely slept at all. Again and again she went over the options for conversation, which seats each of them ought to take around the table, the outfit she would wear, what impression she should give Steve, what gestures to avoid making, with which smile to assent.

She got up before the sun was up. She bathed quickly, brushed her teeth, opened the refrigerator and took a drink of Coca-Cola. The long white dress, the strappy sandals, and a touch of perfume behind her ears. That was all. Simple, light, the ideal attire for a breakfast with a view of the lake. Silvi had left it out on the chair and took less than a second to put it on. There could be no question of a necklace, nor earrings – just a hint of lipstick. She examined herself in the mirror and could not have been more pleased.

She ran into Helmut as he was coming out of the garage.

Where are you off to at this hour? asked Helmut.

I've got something important, Silvi said.

Did you buy those shoes?

Sure, said Silvi and got on her bicycle. The day before she'd made certain that the tyres were fully inflated and that the chain was properly oiled.

She soared down the hillside as fast as she could go. The streets empty and still in shadow, the mountain air on her arms, her hair afloat, her legs slick, smooth, the skirt of her dress gathered so it wouldn't get caught in the spokes. She went along the river, took the main street, crossed the city and, riding on the wrong side of the street, reached the curve that came out onto the hardware store. She got off her bike and dragged it down the alley. In the back the little patio was covered in pots of dry dirt. The window of the flat where Bob and Steve lived was still shut. Silvi rested her bike against the wall and knocked on the door. Once. Twice. Silence. She looked at her watch, it was seven-twenty-eight. She knocked again. She thought she heard, from the other side, a grunt, an elastic snap, a slight rustling of cloth.

Who is it? asked a voice she thought must be Bob's.

It's me, Silvi!

Just a minute.

Silvi heard whispering and hasty footsteps. The noise of a drawer being opened. More whispering, and then, at last, the key being turned in the lock.

Bob had on a pair of trousers like basketball players wear and a T-shirt two or three sizes too big. His hair was matted, messy.

Ready for breakfast? said Silvi, glancing inside through the half-open door. She saw a Formica table, dirty plates, a stack of Books of Mormon, some cracker packets, and a sugar bowl without its lid on. She saw two plastic chairs bearing the logo of Quilmes beer. She saw a poster of Jesus' face nailed to the wall and, underneath the poster, a twin-sized bed, its sheets hanging off it, a pillow crumpled into its headboard.

What time is it? said Bob, scratching his head.

Seven-thirty, Silvi said.

Behind Bob, sitting on the bed, in his boxers and also wearing an enormous T-shirt over his chest, Silvi could just make out Steve. He was yawning and rubbing his eyes.

Hey! Silvi said to him, peeping in.

Steve put a baseball cap on backward and smiled at her, giving her a wave.

We'll need about fifteen minutes, said Bob.

That's OK, no problem, I'll just be out here.

Great, said Bob and shut the door.

Only then did Silvi notice the tide of stench that had come out of the flat. It smelled similar to sweat, but it was more intense, blended with the remnants of sleep, dry saliva, dirty sheets, and something sweeter, old apples or cereal gone bad or a piece of cake forgotten in the fridge.

Silvi closed her eyes and took a deep breath.

This was Steve's true aroma, she said to herself, bursting with joy. The Axe Apollo was nothing more than a disguise he used on other people.

11

Despite the fact that Silvi explained to them, multiple times, that they could go back to the buffet as often as they wanted, Bob and Steve only served themselves a cup of milk and one piece of bread each.

There weren't many people in the dining room. Four or five tourists who came down looking sleepy and took pictures of the view and of the dining room and served themselves oversized helpings of eggs and sausage. And Bob and Steve right there, in front of Silvi, with their ties and white shirts, gel in their hair, parted to one side, their backpacks filled with Books of Mormon, their skin coated in Axe.

Outside, on the lake, a windsurfer's sail cut the surface of the water in two as it glided so slowly it looked stationary.

You can go back, said Silvi. Get as much as you want.

This will be fine, Bob said and took his seat.

Oh, sorry, said Silvi. That seat's for Steve. You can sit in the other one.

Bob and Steve exchanged a look. Without a word Steve took the seat Silvi had designated for him. She tried to start up a conversation. She talked about the weather, about how great the hardware store was – the one they lived behind – and praised the quality of the scrambled eggs, of the bacon, said that if they wanted pancakes they just had to request them.

We're good, Bob said.

Before we get started, said Steve, we wanted to apologize for this morning. We almost never forget things that way. And we also wanted to tell you that we think you're very brave for everything you're doing. Your calling is strong, come what may, we're very proud of you. We want to you to know that.

Yes, yes, said Silvi.

Bob cleared his throat.

Alright, let's get started, he said. We'd like to share the Gospel with you first, he said as he took a Bible out of his backpack and set it open on the table. Silvi, I'll ask you to read from here to here.

The passage in question was from the New Testament. Jesus was talking to his disciples, who were seated on a lakeshore. Silvi knew this passage, had heard it a million times, but she still got tripped up reading it and had to start over. She wasn't really paying attention to the words. As often as she could she looked up at Steve. Steve's broad smile, the white light from the big window showing his head in relief, a little bit of stubble reflecting the sun on his badly shaved cheek. Silvi messed up again, at around the same spot as before. Bob fidgeted in his seat. Silvi started over, again. Jesus was saying to the Apostles that they should... Silvi finished the paragraph as best she could and gave the Bible back to Bob.

Alright, he said. So what's this verse about?

What? said Silvi.

Bob's fingers drummed the tablecloth.

What's it about? he said. What you just read.

Silvi didn't know how to respond. She looked at Steve and smiled, but Steve did not smile back. Suddenly he was very serious, more so than Silvi had ever seen him.

Bob sighed and leaned back.

OK, he said. That's enough, he said. I'm going to ask you a question that I need for you to answer honestly.

Sure, said Silvi.

Are you actually interested in becoming a Mormon, or do you just want to be around us?

Silvi felt the heat rising to her face.

Of course I'm interested...

We need the truth, Silvi, Steve said then.

Silvi looked down, at her hands, and said nothing.

Alright, said Bob. I see. We're going to cut our losses here. We've given this a lot of thought, and this is going to be the best solution. As of tomorrow Steve will have been transferred to another city, far away from here.

Silvi started, looked back up.

I don't understand, she said.

Steve is leaving. Today, said Bob. He'll proceed with his mission somewhere else. He'll go this very evening. His presence here puts obstacles along our path to salvation, and his transfer will be best for everyone involved.

Steve had turned to look out the big window. He gazed into the distance, at some point in the middle of the lake.

Is this true? Silvi asked him.

Steve, answer me, is this true?

We've already made the decision, said Bob. Steve's got to go.

Can he do that? Steve? Can he...?

Yes, said Steve, without turning his head. It will be best for everyone. I've got to go.

Steve had said yes.

To Silvi it seemed that all the water in the lake was disappearing, that the sun was going out, that a black hand was pulling downwards from the inside of her throat and ripping off her eyelids. She swallowed, trying to seem fine.

Could you leave us alone for a moment? she asked Bob. I'd like to speak with Steve.

I'm afraid that's not possible, said Bob. Missionaries always go in pairs. It's one way we have of repelling the devil's attacks.

Alright, Bob, said Steve.

But.

It's OK, Bob, I'll be fine. Just give us a minute. I think I should talk to her.

Bob hesitated, but he finally stepped away, in silence.

None of the topics of conversation that Silvi had practiced over and over all night would do now, and nonetheless they were all still there, orbiting around in her mind, getting jumbled up together, preventing her from thinking clearly.

Silvi closed her eyes.

She could feel an infinitesimal vibration that passed through her whole body, her skin trembling.

You can't leave, she said. You can't leave.

Steve pulled his chair up over the rug and came closer to Silvi. He leaned in, rested his elbows on his knees so his eyes were level with Silvi's.

Silvi, look at me, listen to me, he said. Do you really want to be a Mormon?

Silvi looked up. Steve's body was right there, so close. The smell of his Axe Apollo, and beneath it, his smell, pure smell, sweet and peppery, the smell of Steve stripped down.

No, she said. I'm not interested in becoming a Mormon, she said, and she sought out his gaze, wetting her lips so she could kiss him.

Steve smiled sadly and moved her away.

I'm sorry, said Silvi. I thought you liked me back... I thought we'd leave together and go somewhere far away. Far away from everything, just you and me, somewhere else.

Silvi, listen, please, said Steve, taking her hand.

You're all mixed up, he said. You can't run away. No matter how many different cities and countries and continents you go to, you'll never be able to escape, he said. Nobody runs away from God.

His warm hand, soft, as though covered in talcum powder. His eyes lighting her all up in pale blue, brilliant. His perfect beauty, ancient, calm.

You need faith, said Steve. You are searching for it, that I see.

Silvi covered her mouth, but her eyes filled with tears.

Bob is right, the best thing for me to do now is go, said Steve. But that doesn't matter. We can't let it matter. I believe this meeting is a sign from God.

But I love you, said Silvi.

No, you don't, said Steve. It's not me you love, he said.

You'll see what I mean down the road, he said. It's all a matter of time. You'll see.

12

The first thing Silvi did was change the sheets, wash the pillows, throw the Axe in the bin. Then she shut herself in her room, lowered the shades all the way, turned off the light. She spent an entire day this way. Then another.

Are you alright, sweetheart? Alba Clara would ask every so often from the hall.

Silvi couldn't hear her. She was burying her sobs by biting the blanket. She couldn't stop thinking about Steve, but every time she closed her eyes the people who showed up were all the dying ones she had ever attended. The old lady who'd been over ninety and lost all of her teeth who, when Alba Clara had finished putting the oil on her, had asked her to draw an extra cross on her forehead.

I'll rest easier that way, she'd said.

You don't need it, you're good now, Alba Clara had said.

You're sure one is enough? Go on, do another one, what's it going to cost you.

The skinny woman – so skinny – sleeping in fits and starts lying in bed with a sunken face, just eyes and those long arms. Beside the bed, on a tall nightstand, there were a bunch of jars with plant cuttings: jasmines sprouting roots, silver vines, geraniums, hibiscus, a few handfuls of grass, just ordinary lawn grass, from the street, the little blades stretching upwards, the naked roots floating. The woman had opened her eyes and spent a moment looking at the water in the jars. She seemed to be waking up from a dream, not understanding where she was. She blinked a few times, turned towards them, her eyes running over Alba Clara's hands, the capsule, the case, the jar.

Laura, these are the women from the church, someone had said from behind them. They've come to give you...

Then the woman sat up and took in a big mouthful of air. Her eyes focused, the kerchief that had been covering her head slipped back, revealing greying fluff.

Get out! she'd screamed.

Get out of here, she'd screamed, bending towards them with her mouth open wide, her teeth looming, gleaming.

But above all, the one Silvi remembered was the boy from the hospital. Time and again she went back to that afternoon when she'd slipped out of school and gone down the hospital hallways, alone, until she'd reached intensive care. The nurses knew her, and she had easily managed to talk them into letting her see him. The plastic tube climbing up to his mouth. His body covered in the green sheet, his eyes swollen, open but still, his damp hair that fell backward, the little valley of hair in the middle of his chest. He was the most beautiful boy Silvi had ever seen. His chin had a gash in it. A neat cut, clean, the ripped up skin visible and underneath it a thin layer of fat and the cleft in the open flesh. With the tip of her finger Silvi had pressed at its edge. The boy hadn't moved. A red grid had appeared in the yellow fat, but no blood had spurted out.

The next day, when Silvi had tried to go back, the nurses informed her that the boy had died.

13

Alba Clara asked Helmut to get Father Sampacho and bring him back in the car.

Leave her alone, Helmut told her. She's not a little kid anymore, she's all grown up now. Let her do as she pleases.

You listen to me, said Alba Clara. This is serious. Go get Father Sampacho.

Even though it was still just January, hot, Father

Sampacho arrived wrapped up in his thickest coat and with a hat on. Helmut had to help him out of the car and make sure he didn't trip on the kerb. Father Sampacho took tiny steps, leaning on his cane with the three feet, and he took forever to cross the dried out lawn.

If her room is upstairs I won't be able to get up there, he said when he got inside.

She's down here, don't worry, Alba Clara answered.

Father Sampacho sighed with relief, took off his hat and asked for a glass of water. He drank it all in one gulp, standing up, in the kitchen.

Have you been praying? he asked Alba Clara.

She nodded.

Good, good. Alright, let's go and see her.

Alba Clara walked him down the hallway, and Father Sampacho leaned against Silvi's door and said her name twice, hitting the door with his whole palm.

Silvi, my dear, are you alright? he asked in his worn-out voice.

On the other side of the door there was only silence. Father Sampacho tried again.

What's going on, Silvi? Talk to me. It's alright if you've become a Mormon.

Leave me alone, all of you! Leave me alone! Silvi screamed from inside her room, and Father Sampacho raised his eyebrows.

Tell her to open the door, tell her she has to come out, Alba Clara whispered to him.

Silvi, just let me in for a second, Father Sampacho said. There's nothing you can't talk to me about. Open the door and we'll pray together, the Lord in all his wisdom will come to your aid.

A resounding thud against the door made him reel back. Silvi had thrown something.

Ah! The worst of the dark night! Father Sampacho

said afterwards, sitting down at the table.

The darkest hours! The deepest darkness! he said as he stirred his tea with a little spoon.

This won't last long. It will pass. Soon, soon, said Father Sampacho. You just have to pray as much as you can, ask God to tend to her. I know what I'm talking about, the dawn will be here soon, he said, dipping a bit of bread into his mug.

14

On the third day she spent locked in her room, Silvi put on her blue dress, pulled her hair back into a bun and applied makeup to her eyes, cheeks, lips. She grabbed a pair of Alba Clara's high heels, and she climbed out the window once the siesta was well underway. She went off to one of the bars behind the casino, along the water. She sat at one of the tables in the back, ordered a coffee with milk. From a neighbouring table a man watched her insistently. He was not attractive. He must have been around fifty years old, not a lot of hair, his skin very tanned. Silvi smiled at him. Without taking his eyes off her, the man signalled to the waiter and whispered something into his ear. The waiter nodded. Then he walked over to Silvi's table.

That man wants to buy you a drink, he told her.

Wonderful, said Silvi, and she smiled again.

Sorry, said the waiter softly, are you a whore?

Silvi shook her head.

If you are, I can't let you work here, the waiter said.

I'm not, said Silvi.

So what are you doing here?

What's it to you?

The waiter stepped away.

Silvi smoothed her hair, looked at her nails, finished her coffee.

The man from the neighbouring table walked up to her and sat down.

What would you like? Rum? Whisky?

A Sprite, said Silvi.

The man's breath smelled of tobacco, and he was wearing a cologne that clung to everything, heavily spiced.

I'm a virgin, Silvi told him, and I want to have sex.

Alright, said the man. I can help you with that.

Call off the Sprite, said Silvi. We don't need it.

The man put his hand in his pocket, took out a wad of bills, counted out four or five and dropped them onto the table. Then he wrapped his arm around her waist.

Where would you like to go? he asked as they stepped outside.

To the Lakefront Hotel, said Silvi.

The man frowned.

That one's expensive, he said. Let me take you to another one I know.

He took her to an hourly motel by the side of the highway, close to the exit. They drove right in. The man took off his clothes and waited for her to do the same.

Come here, the man said. Suck my dick until it's hard.

Silvi did as he said.

His pubic hair tickled her nose, and she sneezed.

Bless you, said the man, squeezing her breasts. Then he moved his hands downwards and checked with his fingers.

You're wet, he said.

Yes, Silvi murmured.

Get on your hands and knees.

The man put on a condom and positioned himself behind her. Silvi felt him rest the hot tip of his penis against her without yet putting it inside her. The man kept still. He was breathing heavily, the air felt dense, the flowers brown on the walls, in the wallpaper.

You want me to put it inside you? the man asked in a hoarse voice.

Yes, said Silvi.

Tell me what you want, said the man.

Put it inside me.

Put what?

Put it in.

What?

Your cock, said Silvi.

Where?

In my vagina.

Tell me to put it in your cunt.

Put it in my cunt, said Silvi.

The man barrelled into her and Silvi let out a sob of pain.

Feel that? asked the man.

Yes.

You like it like that, nice and hard.

Silvi couldn't speak.

Do you like it or not?

Yes, said Silvi.

Tell me you like it, tell me, said the man.

I like it, said Silvi as the man took her hips in his hands and began moving backward and forward.

Tell me you like it, the man ordered, louder now.

Silvi could smell his sweat emerging from under his cologne. It was a sour sweat, highly concentrated. The man became more tense with every movement, perspiration falling like rain onto her back.

I like that, I like it, I love it, said Silvi and raised her head and looked back at him over her shoulder. She saw the man's face, an effortful grimace tightening his expression.

Fuck me, Silvi said then. Fuck me, she said, and suddenly it was as if a wave were raising her, lifting her up and displaying her there in the air, in the mixture of aromas in the air.

Her body now weighed nothing, taking off from the bedspread and the floor. Silvi spread into a breath, a howl, a cry. A long moan took her mouth, gasps getting tangled up in her hair. Silvi was floating very high up, with wind all around her, until the man collapsed onto her back, and she felt him crushing her body under his.

Then it was like waking up. Shivers, and Silvi returned to herself again, as though after a long while. It took her time to recognise the hotel room, the cheap curtains, the monotonous rumble of the air conditioner. She arched her back, took a deep breath, brushed back the hair that had stuck to her face.

Go ahead and get cleaned up, the man told her as he removed the condom and tossed it underneath the bed.

15

Irma Bustelo passed away, I heard a little while ago, said Alba Clara when Silvi got home again.

Silvi nodded, opened the refrigerator, poured herself a glass of water.

I'm going to the wake now, they're burying her tomorrow. Do you want me to tell Danilo anything for you?

Who?

Danilo, Irma's son.

Ah, said Silvi. No thanks. No need.

Alba Clara sighed, resigned.

Where's Dad? asked Silvi.

In the garage.

Silvi went to the door and peeked inside and saw him hunched over the table, applying glue to a tiny piece of wood, looking at everything through a magnifying glass under the lamp.

How's that plane coming along? she asked him.

Helmut straightened up. He took off his glasses.

Kid, he said, you're out of your room.

Yep, I'm out.

I'm glad.

Silvi smiled.

So, how's the plane coming along? Is it ready yet? she asked.

Just about, said Helmut.

Are you going to take it on a test flight?

Tomorrow morning, soon as it's light.

Can I go with you?

Of course you can.

When they left, the blue air of the night hadn't yet finished dissolving. Helmut drove with the window open and his elbow resting on the frame. He seemed happy, whistling. He went along the lake until they came to the dam, and then he went up the hill and through the pine trees, over to the other side. From there you could see the full spread of the plain, empty and calm. An azure haze blurred the horizon. The sun was coming up in the distance, barely a reddish phosphorescence just beginning to glow the air. They went down the road with a million curves in it, and, when they reached the flatland, Helmut turned off onto a dirt road you almost wouldn't notice in among the weeds and squat plants. They went all the way down the road until there was nothing recognizable in their surroundings, just the mountains to their backs. The gleaming sun of dawn shone across the tall slopes. Helmut turned off the motor. The sunlight skipped off the rocks and covered them in golden nectar. Helmut opened up the boot, and Silvi helped him take the plane out. The wings were the same size as her outstretched arms and wrapped in bands that made blue, red and white stripes. The remote control was as big as a battery-operated radio and had a big antenna. To the tip of the antenna Helmut had attached a red band.

Helmut placed the plane on the ground.

There aren't any stones, said Silvi.

No, said Helmut. Not out here.

He was holding the remote, moving the controls around.

The rumble started as a stutter, and then the propellers spun and the rumble increased, growing stronger and stronger until it was sustained, constant. Helmut made it accelerate, and the plane taxied over the loose earth. Its casters raised a cloud of dust that was almost invisible, and the plane bucked, unstable, reproducing in its tail and wings every unevenness in the land. The engine pushed harder, its noise becoming sharp and at maximum strength, and its body straightened out, as though scenting the wind, until it took off. The plane rocked slightly but soon stabilized and rose. Helmut guided it with careful movements. His eyes were fixed on it, and his hands on the controls. Silvi sat down on the edge of the hill, hugging her knees, watching the plane get smaller in the sky, its purr farther and farther away, moving towards the sun, until it was no more than a black point in the distance, on the verge of invisibility at the edge of the plain.

How will it get back? asked Silvi when the plane disappeared, fully devoured by the light and the distance.

What if it gets lost? asked Silvi. How's it going to know we're here?

Helmut smiled. Then he opened his arms, wide.

Take a look at all of this, he said. Isn't it swell?

Yes, said Silvi.

No, no, pay attention, he said. Take a good look. Isn't it swell?

Yes, yes, said Silvi.

Helmut nodded, looked down, pursed his lips.

Don't you worry, he said. It'll come back, he said. It'll find us.

A PERFECT CEMETERY

He had the address written down in his planner but didn't need to check: the town had only one hotel, facing the plaza.

A big pink woman crammed into a dress covered in enormous flowers came out to receive him.

Mr Bagiardelli, welcome! she said and hugged him.

I'm Elvita, the owner, she said then, and, there in the middle of the pavement, she hugged him again. Soon she had pulled his suitcase out of the truck.

Fidel! Fidel! she shouted into the lobby. Mr Bagiardelli is here!

Fidel was a boy of no more than ten years old. Elvita passed him the suitcase and the boy dragged it across the patio of large red tiles and ferns in pots.

Here you are, said Elvita, showing him his room: two narrow beds with green covers, cream-coloured walls, a chair to put his clothes on, a lamp without its shade and a dark table underneath the window.

I left you three blankets in the wardrobe. It gets pretty cold here at night.

Víctor Bagiardelli gave a nod. He closed the door, took off his shoes and lay down atop a bed. Its elastic crackled. The mattress was too soft.

But right away there came a knocking at the door. The mayor was there. Fidel had run to the town hall to let him know.

Víctor Bagiardelli had never seen the mayor before; based on his voice over the phone he had pictured him as tall and corpulent, with slumped shoulders. As soon as he opened the door he was able to confirm this hypothesis. The mayor was stocky and had a flabby face. Víctor Bagiardelli was surprised by his black hair, pulled back, wavy, without a speck of grey. He couldn't quite tell if it was a toupee or if the mayor just dyed his hair.

Welcome, said Mayor Giraudo and held out his hand. Do you have a minute? I'd let you rest but it'll get dark on us before long.

Víctor Bagiardelli gave a nod.

Just give me a second, and I'll get my notebook.

Of course, answered Giraudo.

Víctor Bagiardelli closed the door to his room, sat down on the edge of the bed and let exactly ten minutes go by. Then he strode out towards reception.

The town was called Colonel Isabeta. It was wedged into the edge of the prairie, at the very end where the sierra began. To the west it faced the mountains, its final dwellings climbing up into their foothills. From the east it was battered by the wind from the plains. The trees of the public spaces were limited to evergreens, pruned so their branches wouldn't graze the cables of the power lines. Now they were coming to the last of the afternoon. It hadn't really begun to get dark yet, but the cold already required zipped-up jackets and tightly pulled scarves. Mayor Giraudo hustled along with his fingers inter-locking over the small of his back; Víctor Bagiardelli followed him without a word. They cut across the plaza in a diagonal line and headed up a street that rose towards the mountains. Two blocks along, the mayor came to a stop before a house, gesturing for Víctor Bagiardelli to go inside. The door was unlocked. Inside, sitting at a table covered with an oilcloth, a woman was reading a magazine. Giraudo greeted her with a nod and continued down the hallway. The woman watched them pass her by and went back to her reading. There was no noise inside the house, the shades were all drawn and most of the rooms rested in torpid shadow. The smell of Creolin and just-washed floors rose from the baseboards and overpowered other smells that were slighter, barely penetrating the walls: hints of soup, damp wool, and cat piss. In the hall there were cross-stitched wall hangings and old photographs of smiling babies and first communions. At its end a fluorescent bulb flickered over little bathroom tiles. The white gleam of it slipped into the adjoining bedroom and lit up a rectangle over large tiles and the legs of a hospital bed. Mayor Giraudo plunged into the darkness of the room. For a second, Víctor Bagiardelli lost sight of him; then Giraudo switched on a small lamp, half-covered by a handkerchief.

A very old man was sleeping on his back, barely even weighing down the sheets. He looked more like a bird. His body was small and frail: his shoulders narrow, his head enormous. Without any dental support, his lips sank inwards, creating a deep, dark hollow. He didn't have any hair left, just a tiny bit of fluff on the sides, framing his calloused and disproportionate ears. His naked head was splattered in age spots that intermingled, ochre and maroon, leaving not a single centimetre of unoccupied skin.

Giraudo went up to the bed, lowered his head and then stayed there, his pupils fixed on the covers draped over the old man. The old man's breathing was almost imperceptible, a faint and distant rasp, but it was the only thing that could be heard in the whole house. That and the pages of the newspaper the woman turned over and over in the kitchen.

Relative of yours? said Víctor Bagiardelli. Something in the arrangement of the eyebrows, the variety of nose, had suggested this idea.

He's my dad, said the mayor, without taking his eyes off the covers on the bed.

How old?

A hundred and four.

How long has he been here for?

Three weeks, ever since he broke his hip.

What's the prognosis?

Well, they won't operate on him. He's got an infection.

What's his name?

Hipólito.

Víctor Bagiardelli knelt so that his head was at pillow level, his mouth very near the old man's face. He took in his own hands the old man's fingers, knotted like acacia branches. His nails were thick and grooved, and the way they stuck out they seemed almost ready to come off.

Stay strong, Hipólito, whispered Víctor Bagiardelli in the old man's furry ear.

Stay strong, Hipólito, he repeated. At least until spring. I'm going to create the most beautiful cemetery you've ever laid eyes on. I'm going to build you a perfect cemetery.

From the other side of the bed the mayor nodded. His eyes were filled with tears. When Víctor Bagiardelli stood back up, Giraudo had already dried them, but a faint red line still marred the edges of his eyelids.

Víctor Bagiardelli clapped him on the back.

You can count on me, he said. I'm the best.

Giraudo gulped, then pulled himself together.

That's why I called you, he said, under his breath.

At this the old man coughed. Once. Twice. Three times. Then he opened his eyes, cleared his throat, sat straight up and spat to one side onto the floor of the bedroom.

Hang on, said Víctor Bagiardelli. Wasn't he at death's door?

Who, Pops? said the mayor.

The old man surveyed them with the hard, mistrustful eyes of a falcon.

Who the hell is this? he said.

Víctor Bagiardelli looked at the mayor. The mayor looked at Víctor Bagiardelli.

He's an engineer, said the mayor.

What do I want an engineer for?

The mayor looked at Bagiardelli.

Bagiardelli shrugged.

It's for your prosthesis, Pops, said Giraudo. He's come to town to design your prosthesis.

Out of aluminium?

No, Dad, said the mayor. Only the best, stainless steel.

When's the operation?

Come on, Pops! Where's the fire? They've got to make it first.

Have you watered the garden yet?

The nurse is in charge of that.

My parsley'll all dry up. That woman is good for nothing. What about the chickens? Have you fed the chickens?

Yes, Pops, said the mayor.

Open the blinds for me, would you? I'd like a little sunshine.

It's almost dark, Dad.

And although you had all day you didn't have a moment to simply water my parsley, now did you?

I really didn't, Dad.

Stuff and nonsense! said Old Man Giraudo. Stuff and nonsense!

The next day Miss Mahoney, the mayor's secretary, took him over the land. She was a tall woman, somewhat equine, with wide hips and sizeable teeth shaped like ice lollies. She wore her hair very short, curly, and a brown tailored suit with a necklace of red beads around her neck.

It's a shame we've never had a cemetery, all these years, she said. All those wonderful people we just gave to Deheza when they died. People who did things for our town, who had real attributes, who won awards.

Deheza was the next town over, less than ten kilometres away, along the sierra.

How is it no one ever thought of this before? said Víctor Bagiardelli.

Miss Mahoney shrugged.

Laziness, she said. Or habit. People here are just used to sending their dead to Deheza. It wouldn't occur to them to make a change. That's how they are.

They were walking up the hill, towards the end of one of the dirt streets. There weren't any homes around, just vacant lots and the loose rocks of the sloping road bearing them upward. It was a clear morning, dry, cold but sunlit, the sky transparent.

All this, all the way up, up to the mountain's edge, is municipal land, said Miss Mahoney. So anywhere that strikes your fancy's yours.

Low and shaggy vegetation lay over the hillside like a fuzzy, frizzy blanket. It was all espinillos covered in lichen and scrub.

Víctor Bagiardelli turned and looked out over the plain. Colonel Isabeta rolled out beneath his feet, down the hill: the faded roofs, the clumsy trees, the church bell tower. On the other side of the town, the road agleam, two cars that sped by, heading to Deheza. Beyond, the plain, sectioned up into pasture, and at the limit of the desert air the vanishing horizon, dispersing into vapour, an undulating distance.

An oak, said Víctor Bagiardelli. An oak tree up top, and underneath the oak a nice wide bench, for people to sit and take in the community of the living, their dwellings, the landscape. The infinite, where your eyes get lost and everything seems to end – but doesn't.

In his mind's eye he could already see the new cemetery. The site could not have been better – he would never encounter its equal. He opened his notebook and drew a quick sketch. He inspected the land while nibbling on the tip of his pencil and listing his ideas aloud. He passed through groups of little chañar trees and paid no mind to their thorns as they scratched him. Wisps of panicles and bracts latched onto the fabric of his shirt without him noticing. Thistle clung to his trouser legs, but he didn't care. His walking raised a dust cloud that made him sneeze. Víctor Bagiardelli stood at the very top of the hill and there, standing still, his notebook wedged into his armpit, his hands folded behind him, he squinted and tried to focus on the horizon. He resumed his sketching. With his index finger and thumb he made a framing square that contained the landscape. He extended his arms to get the proportions; he took notes; he muttered exclamations. In the air his pupils traced his imagined cemetery.

A boulevard lined with plantain trees that stretches from the entrance gate to a chapel with white walls, he said, and Miss Mahoney nodded.

Paths with S-shaped curves. To the north, a little patchwork of candelabra trees and monkey puzzles that will open out like parasols. Agapanthus, agapanthus, lots of azaleas, but above all agapanthus. And on that gentle hillside there, a covering of green where the graves can go in right at ground level.

Miss Mahoney gazed at him, enraptured.

Down below, in the ravine, a garden of white roses for the departed children, and the unborn. And the ossuary in that corner there, between quaking aspens that will whisper it quiet and frame it. Past that, a row of beech and magnolia trees to orient the eyes. And over here, my masterstroke, a sweeping semicircle of weeping willows, so that its curtain will fall all the way to the ground and on days with a breeze caress the headstones with its tips.

That'll be so nice, said Miss Mahoney. I knew you were the best, she said. Then she dragged Víctor Bagiardelli off to the town hall.

They went straight to the mayor's office.

What about my dad? asked Giraudo when the designer had finished detailing his plans. Where will we put my pops?

Underneath the oak tree, next to the bench, responded Víctor Bagiardelli.

Out of the whole place, will that be the absolute best spot? asked the mayor.

I can assure you it will be. It will be the focal point that will capture everyone's attention. The pinnacle.

Nothing but the best, nodded the mayor and began inquiring into the budgets and fees. In order to oversee the work on the cemetery, Víctor Bagiardelli would be willing to spend the winter in the town, but that would mean paying him an amount four times heftier than what he would have charged for the design alone. On the other hand, the mayor would save money on the execution, because almost everything could be done with city employees, with a little help from local labour. When the time came to buy the trees, Víctor Bagiardelli promised to get them a discount at a couple of the nurseries he always used.

The only issue is the bulldozer to get rid of the hill,

said the mayor. Deheza has one, but no way I'll go to them.

We can rent one, suggested Miss Mahoney.

Which will add to the budget.

You'll get nothing for free in this life, said Víctor Bagardelli. Although for you, for your town, because I feel this hillside has exceptional potential, I will make a small personal sacrifice and give you a little discount on my fees.

They went back to adding and subtracting and in less than fifteen minutes had arrived at an agreement.

Now we just need to get the town council to approve it. Let's go and have a talk with Romero, said the mayor and got up from his desk and put on his jacket.

Again they crossed the plaza diagonally. Romero was an auto mechanic, and they found him lying on the floor, face up, underneath a blue truck that was losing oil.

This is Romero, head of the council, said Mayor Giraudo.

I object, said Romero as he scrambled up.

To what?

The cemetery.

Why?

Principle, said Romero.

Where is it you're planning on putting your loved ones when they're gone?

It's just me, I'm on my own. My father — rest in peace — and my mother — rest in peace — are already in Deheza.

But what about the common good? the mayor protested.

Your own good, you mean. It's your old man that wants a grave, said Romero.

The mayor snorted twice, turned on his heels and stalked off without another word. Víctor Bagiardelli followed him in silence.

You see what I'm up against? said the mayor once they were back in the town hall. A bunch of ignoramuses who care nothing for progress. It's their fault we're in the boat we're in. It was the same with the proposal to divert the stream and create a spa, to develop our tourist industry. They shot it down because they figured it'd just be too much trouble. Do you have any idea how our economy would be flourishing now if we had a spa? The jobs alone. But this time I won't let them win. I'll hold a referendum. Miss Mahoney! he shouted. Get me Monetti on the line. He's the one with the loudspeaker. He and I'll have a little chat.

That same afternoon, a ramshackle Renault 12 cruised up and down the streets of Colonel Isabeta, methodically. Two speakers attached to the luggage rack proclaimed the referendum, scheduled for the following Sunday, while simultaneously promoting the concept of a cemetery of the town's very own and urging voters to stop burying their dead in Deheza. They are our deceased, and we want them close to home! screeched the recorded voice of the mayor again and again as dusk descended over the town.

We need to hurry, the mayor whispered to him the morning they broke ground and laid the cornerstone. We need to hurry, he said. The doctor suspects the infection may be spreading. He doesn't think my pops will last more than a couple of months.

I don't know if we'll be able to open the cemetery that soon, said Víctor Bagiardelli.

Do everything you can. I'm not about to put him in Deheza, said the mayor and floated off in a cloud of other men from the town hall.

The plan was to attack the hill on several fronts at once. The first step was to create a path for the truck to carry bricks and bags of cement up to the embankment where two masons and a master builder were already digging where the chapel's foundations would go. Meanwhile a crew of town employees would put up the perimeter wall while another started clearing the area by hand, advancing over the scrub from below, using scythes in parts with solid weeds, chains and chainsaws for the trees that might give the bulldozer trouble. Víctor Bagiardelli, meanwhile, set up his drafting table in the middle of the street, right at the base of the hill, facing where eventually they would erect the entrance gate that would nightly divide the living from the dead. From there, standing in the weak light of winter and shielding his eyes with his hand, he would give orders and contemplate the terrain of this, his latest cemetery. He would study it, memorize it, until it was fully his own. He'd close his eyes and just briefly, as he waited for his ideas to decant, he would nibble on the tip of his pencil. Then, as though waking back up from a dream, he would open his eyes and with no hesitation, in quick bold lines, he would sketch the paths to be traversed by the mourners, the arboreal islets that would provide them shade, the flowerbeds to mitigate their sorrow.

Miss Mahoney came by a couple of times a day to see how things were going and convey messages or suggestions.

The mayor would really like for you to visit his father, she told him one morning. But you need to keep up appearances insofar as his hip surgery's concerned. Here, take this tape and pretend like you're taking his measurements.

You all still haven't told him the truth? said Víctor Bagiardelli.

Miss Mahoney shrugged.

That's just how they are, she said. At this stage, there's no sense trying to change them.

Old Man Giraudo was in bed, leaning up against three fluffy pillows. His arms, resting atop his blankets, were just long bones encased in shabby leather. The whites of his eyes were now yellow, clouded by phlegm.

I've been expecting you for some time, was the first thing he said. He looked like he was just waking back up.

Víctor Bagiardelli was on the verge of extracting the measuring tape from his pocket, but the mayor's father stopped him.

Come, have a seat here, he said. We've got more gossips in this town than Christians. I know exactly who you are. So now tell me the truth, do you have a nice place picked out for me to be buried?

The nicest spot of all. Your son wants the very best for you.

Describe it to me, will you?

There will be an oak, a great oak, leafy, wide, at least fifteen, maybe twenty years old and as tall as a three-story house. That concerns me a bit, finding the right one. But with a little luck we'll get it.

Why would it concern you?

It's not easy to get an oak at that age that's available for transplant.

A grown oak, you're saying. How much will a grown oak set you back?

Víctor Bagiardelli gave an amount.

It isn't cheap, I realise, he said. On top of that you've got to figure in the transport and the company that does the transplant itself. You need people who specialise in that — and they do charge for their expertise. But that is unavoidable. We need an oak that has volume. It's going to be the focal point for every visitor, the aesthetic equilibrium of the whole shebang. So you'll rest there, under the oak, in the very best location.

The very best location! Ha! said Old Man Giraudo and opened his mouth wide and let out a guffaw. Víctor Bagiardelli glimpsed the rim of his gums, pink and abandoned. Old Man Giraudo's laughter sounded more like the honking of a goose. His head was too big and heavy for his narrow chest, and soon his laughter had transformed into a long and hacking cough. Old Man Giraudo's shoulders rose as he choked, his tongue protruding.

Víctor Bagiardelli leaned in to try and help him, but the old man fended him off and kept coughing, his face getting redder and redder, until at last the coughing fit was over.

Víctor Bagiardelli offered him a glass of water.

Water only makes it worse, said Old Man Giraudo and he closed his eyes, and for a long while he didn't say another word.

Like I'm going to care whether the location is great or know the age of the oak! he said once his chest had completely finished heaving. The best part is that the town is footing the bill. Oh, I've heard about that, too.

Víctor Bagiardelli didn't know how to respond.

My son can't stand me, said Old Man Giraudo, sighing. I'm a nuisance to him.

I don't think – began Víctor Bagiardelli, but the mayor's father wasn't listening.

He could never stand me, he said. Up to when I turned eighty he hid it well enough – out of respect, I guess. But from eighty to ninety I began to detect his irritation – though I have to admit that back then he was still pretty patient with me. He was probably telling himself I didn't have much time left – that soon enough I'd stop being a pain in his neck. The problems really started when I turned a hundred. At that point he could no longer conceal it. You can see it in his face. I'm nothing but a bother, so far as he's concerned. He can't wait for me to die.

Don't talk that way, your son is – mumbled Víctor Bagiardelli.

No point in your standing up for him, you don't even know him. You don't know what he's capable of. First the geography teacher, now this cemetery, next year it'll be some new notion. They're all just hints.

I don't see what you mean, said Víctor Bagiardelli.

He sent the teacher pretending to be writing a book. Told me they were wanting to come up with an homage. She brought with her one of those machines that record your voice and started asking me year by year what it was I had done with my life. What had I done this year, what had I done that year. But I caught on pretty quick it was a ruse and started telling her I could not recall. She was a tenacious one, however. She kept right on asking me. Three afternoons in a row she pestered me, question after question, until finally I got sick of it and refused to admit her again. You can pronounce the number one-oh-four quick enough, but if you write down every single date it gets clear enough what a long life you've had, what an awfully long life, and that it's high time you were getting on your way. But I'll have you know I won't give him that satisfaction. So there is no sense in you hurrying up with your cemetery, because I am not going to die. Now do you see what I mean?

Víctor Bagiardelli didn't respond.

Now do you see what I mean? Old Man Giraudo asked again.

Alright, alright, said Víctor Bagiardelli.

Very good, said Old Man Giraudo. Now: did you bring me cigarettes?

Víctor Bagiardelli shook his head.

Ah! What a shame. That Miss Mahoney's a good woman, she always brings me cigarettes. Don't you forget next time. It doesn't have to be a whole pack, three or four is fine. Talking of that, when will you come back to see me? How's tomorrow?

The next day Víctor Bagiardelli had to attend a dinner the Society for Development was putting on for him, where he ran into the geography teacher.

He's a difficult man, she said when Víctor Bagiardelli asked her about Old Man Giraudo.

The geography teacher smiled then and made no further comments. They were surrounded by the sounds of silverware striking ceramic, fingers that ambled over a piano, linen napkins lost between chair legs, kisses planted on the rims of crystalware. The evening's hostess was an amiable widow and cultural enthusiast who – as they all listened to the local choir intone a few tunes – came up to the corner where Víctor Bagiardelli had sought refuge and began to praise his works.

It's a real treat to have you here, she whispered in his ear. I have personally experienced your cemeteries in Olaeta and Charras, as well as the one in Villa Granado, and the one in Los Terrales. My husband is buried in Deheza, but I've already decided that as soon as your cemetery is open I'll have him brought back here.

Víctor Bagiardelli gave her a nod of thanks.

Tell me, continued the hostess, resting her hand, which was weighed down with rings, on the cemetery designer's arm. Have you ever considered putting on an exhibition of your sketches and designs?

I can't hardly see that anyone would take an interest in it, responded Víctor Bagiardelli.

Of course they would! I know they would! You just need to work up the courage and put on an exhibition.

They wouldn't be worth all that, he said. The beauty I seek is not the kind you hang up on a wall. Mine is another sort of beauty altogether, one that comforts and envelops, keeps company, consoles.

Gracious! Such wise words! exclaimed the lady of the house.

The enraged eyes of the choir director darted around seeking the source of the racket. They fell silent, permitting the children singing to be the only voices in the room.

For Víctor Bagiardelli, such hobnobbing was a nuisance. All he wanted was to create the most beautiful cemetery anyone had ever seen, and to eat in peace at his hotel, without anyone tormenting him with questions or expecting him to tell humorous anecdotes or say things they'd find profound; without anyone overwhelming him with stories of the town or inquiring as to his opinion of this or that other cemetery. Víctor Bagiardelli wanted to be left alone in his room, with his books, his notebook and his portable cassette tape player. And at the end of the afternoon, as the workers were replacing their tools in their cases and the cemetery hill was slowly emptying, what he wanted was to take a bath, put on a clean shirt and go out for a walk over the open plain, moving away from Colonel Isabeta.

Don't you dilly-dally! Dinner's right at nine! Elvita would shout at him when she saw him leave.

And don't fill up on junk! I'm making ravioli!

Víctor Bagiardelli would strike out east, crossing the highway, climbing over the fence – then it was all pasture, up ahead, nothing but pasture. Dry leaves and stalks of corn and wheat had been plughed deep into the fields and Víctor Bagiardelli would walk along the bare ground, his heavy shoes breaking up the clods of earth, making his way over the plain, further and further, in that wind that huffed at his ears and enveloped his head in a bubble of pure air. The owls watched him go by, keeping track of his movements, rotating their necks. To evade his charge the lapwings would take flight; their shrieks would echo, scattered by that wind. They'd flap their wings a few times and then commit to coasting. Behind him, the sun, which in less than an hour would settle down behind the mountains, now stretched out silhouettes, making them disproportionate: as Víctor Bagiardelli walked he trod on his own shadow. Before him, the horizon was a clean line that got away up ahead of him at every step, a line desired, impossible to reach. Until night caught up with the distance; at the boundary between them, sky and earth were now dissolving into black, and the horizon disappearing into nothingness. So Víctor Bagiardelli would go back into town. Over his head the first stars gleamed; the remains of the day's light phosphoresced out past the mountains, making them stand out. From pastures he could contemplate their majesty. He'd see their soft slopes, the gorges, its passes, its ridge and highest peaks. And, at their foot, the cemetery hill, backdrop to the far-off hamlet. Víctor Bagiardelli could imagine it green, covered in trees, serene and proud. His masterwork, a perfect cemetery.

Winter intensified, nearing its peak, and one icy night as Víctor Bagiardelli dawdled a little longer than he usually did on his walks he glimpsed, as he was returning to the town, the tall, ungainly figure of Miss Mahoney crossing the plaza.

What can you be doing here so late, when it's so cold? He asked her.

Miss Mahoney smiled. She was one of those women who, on smiling, revealed their gums.

I've been at the old man's house, she said, her breath clouding the air.

Something wrong?

She shook her head.

I always go and see him after dinner, just to make sure things are OK with the nurses.

Is that part of your job, as a secretary?

Miss Mahoney made a face without her lips coming apart this time.

The mayor asked me to do it as a personal favour. He can't stand to do it, and I don't mind going and just having a quick look.

The streetlamp on the corner swayed in the wind, its light – orange, amber – illuminating Miss Mahoney's white face. She pulled out a cigarette.

Do you smoke? she offered.

Víctor Bagiardelli shook his head.

Almost without realising, they started walking side by side, until they came to a bench. Miss Mahoney lit her cigarette. Víctor Bagiardelli sat down next to her.

None of this makes that much sense, he said. He asks me to build the best cemetery for his father but the two of them can't even stand each other. If he's about to die, I don't understand why they wouldn't want to spend some time together, say goodbye.

Those two said goodbye a long time ago, said Miss Mahoney. Ever since the old man turned eighty-five, they've been saying goodbye.

I still don't understand, said Víctor Bagiardelli and took the cigarette from Miss Bagiardelli's hands to have a puff.

They never got along well, she said. Sometimes that happens. People who don't see eye to eye.

But then why this whole thing with the cemetery?

Miss Mahoney took back her cigarette. She held in her breath, let the smoke escape little wisps at a time.

To not keep giving Deheza the satisfaction, I suppose. Besides, it's a good idea, the town needs a cemetery. Better to just get it over and done with now.

Víctor Bagiardelli didn't answer. He buried his hands in the pockets of his overcoat and sank his neck down between the raised flaps of its collar.

I'm the one who recommended you, don't know if you ever knew that, Miss Mahoney continued. You designed the cemetery where my mum is buried. Parque del Recuerdo, in Admiral Costanzo.

Sector? said Víctor Bagiardelli.

Sector 4, grave 4076, said Miss Mahoney and tossed away her cigarette.

In front of the semicircle of willows, said Víctor Bagiardelli. Over to the left there's a small cluster of pine trees and blue cedars, and on either side of the path, lilies and yellow irises.

Yes, that's it, exactly, said Miss Mahoney.

That's a wonderful place for her, said Víctor Bagiardelli. And in thirty years, once the cedars have grown, it's going to be even more beautiful.

How many cemeteries have you designed? asked Miss Mahoney.

Including this one, forty-eight. But because in the early days lawn cemeteries were all the rage there was also more work to be had. I regret my early cemeteries, though. They're not very good.

Do you remember all of them so well? So clearly?

Every last one, said Víctor Bagiardelli.

Miss Mahoney smiled and leaned into him. She laid her head on his shoulder and turned her face in his direction, seeking him out, eyes closed. Víctor Bagiardelli did nothing. He just waited, until her chapped lips struck his own. He could feel Miss Mahoney's tongue going over the corner of his mouth. It was like a tepid lizard sounding out the morning sun. He opened his mouth and breathed in Miss Mahoney's tobacco breath. It was only a moment. Then Miss Mahoney pulled back and contented herself with just pressing against him, resting her ice-cold cheek in the hollow of his chest.

Víctor Bagiardelli let her be, without moving, and when he felt it had been sufficient, he got up and bade her farewell with a clasp of the hands.

They're waiting for me at the hotel, for dinner, he said, and walked off.

Miss Mahoney remained by herself on the bench.

The next day Víctor Bagiardelli left the town. He needed to go to the city, go around the various nurseries, order the trees and seedlings and seeds for the lawn, and he needed to look for the oak; what worried him most of all was getting a good oak, one that would be able to handle the transplant, so that the inhabitants of Colonel Isabeta wouldn't have to wait, so that from the very start the mayor's father would be able to rest easy in its shade.

A full week he was gone from Colonel Isabeta. When he returned, the truck carrying the bulldozer was awaiting him next to the hill. The whole town had congregated in the frozen orange dawn to see the bulldozer's tracks, balanced on parallel ramps, as it came down.

Goodness gracious, said the mayor. How much is this monster setting us back?

Miss Mahoney trotted after him with an open planner in her hands, gave him an amount. It had four digits in it.

Better finish in a day or our whole budget'll be blown.

Víctor Bagiardelli said the work would not extend beyond what they had planned for. Miss Mahoney avoided his gaze. In fact, at no point did she take her eyes off her planner, taking no interest in the bulldozer on the hill, nor in the people around, nor in the cemetery. When the mayor departed, so did she, without so much as a word.

So Víctor Bagiardelli set up his table in the middle of the street and, as though commanding an orchestra, he began to conduct the movements of the bulldozer. He made it go up and raze the mound. Weeds and spiky branches and vines fell in its path and were crushed. The machine went up and up without stopping, cloaking in smog the scent of the cracked earth and torn roots. The mica veins of the newly exhumed rocks gleamed under the winter sun, and the clumps of roots, which until a second earlier had reached down into the cool darkness of the hill, now overflowed the sides of the front shovel in giant globs. Until, its engine revved, the beast attained the place where the oak would go, at the cemetery's highest point, and Víctor Bagiardelli called it back down, then sent it up again.

By mid-afternoon, the hill had become a smooth convex surface. With it gone, the plots of land made plain to all what the expert eye of Víctor Bagiardelli had long since gleaned. With a wave of his arm, he had the bulldozer back up in the bed of the truck. And he dismissed the village children, who had since morning been sitting on the fine street gravel eating tutuca and watching the bulldozer climb and return.

That's all, folks! Show's over! Víctor Bagiardelli proclaimed.

But the kids paid no attention. Stock still, they watched the bulldozer's tracks being fastened to the truck with three rounds of chain. One of the kids asked the driver if he could climb up onto the bulldozer, just to know how it felt to look out from up there, but the driver wouldn't let him. The truck took off, going slowly, and the kids ran after it. The truck reached the main road, sped up and got further away, becoming smaller and smaller until it disappeared. Then the kids went back to their houses to find out what was for dinner.

Víctor Bagiardelli had designed the entrance gate with thick bars crowned by a stunning frieze. In the drawing, a double knot of iron interrupted each bar at the same level and gave way to a languid candle flame: the same iron, getting thinner as it climbed until at last it evanesced altogether. It was a gate worthy of the cemetery it contained, but he was concerned about the man who would make it, since in Colonel Isabeta there was just one blacksmith, and he was a cousin of Romero's, the head of the town council.

That referendum was a low blow, the blacksmith had told him the first time he went. It was wrong to go over our heads at the council.

He hadn't let him into his shop. He had barely cracked the sheet metal door, then slipped out and talked it over with Víctor Bagiardelli on the pavement.

A job is a job, Enrique, said the blacksmith's wife, peeking her head out from behind him.

Alright, let's see that design, said the blacksmith and took Víctor Bagiardelli's sketches and held them up. He looked them over quickly and passed them to his wife. His grease-stained fingers had marked the pages, so painstakingly prepared.

You can come back in a month for it, he said.

You get what I want here with the spirals? And the frieze, the effect it creates? Víctor Bagiardelli asked. The knots need to function as an allegory of the hardships of life and then, towards the top, there's the ascension.

The blacksmith stared at him a second and went back inside.

Don't you worry, just come back in a month, his wife repeated.

But Víctor Bagiardelli didn't trust him, and every three or four days, before going up the hill, he would pass by his shop with the intention of checking up on the gate's progress, making absolutely sure the blacksmith had fully comprehended his instructions, seeing if in being represented in solid iron the tos and fros he had imagined for the winding top rail would successfully produce the effect he'd had in mind, between elegant and dramatic. The blacksmith's wife would see him on the pavement. All that could be heard of the blacksmith were the blows of his hammer, inside, on red-hot iron. Every time Víctor Bagiardelli tried going inside the shop, the blacksmith's wife would intervene.

Not now, he's busy, and he has a bad temper, she would say. He has to sharpen some ploughshares, and then he's got to finish this harvester shaft.

OK, but the gate? Has he started on the gate yet? Víctor Bagiardelli asked.

You move along, don't you worry, he knows what he's doing, the blacksmith's wife would tell him before she said goodbye. Then Víctor Bagiardelli would leave, and muttering his doubts and his mistrust, he would walk towards the site of the new cemetery, set up his table facing the hill, and shielding his eyes with his hand he would get to monitoring the progress of the soil being fertilized, and the chapel, and the irrigation system and, in general, the work.

But when the wall was almost done and the only thing remaining for the construction of the entrance pillars was the gate, Víctor Bagiardelli decided that the situation could not continue in this way and went to lodge a complaint with the mayor. He waited until Miss Mahoney wasn't inside the Town Hall and expressed his concerns to Giraudo.

I think he's taking longer on purpose, he told him. I think he has some kind of deal with Romero and it's their version of a counterattack.

Who? Enrique? He's in the countermovement, but I don't think he'd do that.

He hasn't even started it yet. He barely even looked at the designs, didn't ask me a single question. He wants to sabotage our cemetery.

He does have his dead resting over in Deheza. And he never goes to visit them... hesitated the mayor. But he's a law-abiding man. If he said a month, it'll take a month.

He's not used to orders like this one, answered Víctor Bagiardelli. I can't ensure the integrity of my work if I have to depend on people like that.

But don't forget he's a very good blacksmith, with excellent training! Didn't they show you the railing he did for old Puchi Actis' place? Take a look at those, and you'll realize. It's the big house at the end of the boulevard. And let me grab Matilda on Sunday on her way out of mass. I'll have a little chat with her. She runs the business and keeps her husband on a tight leash. Now: how long has it been since you went and paid my dad a visit?

I went last week. How's he doing?

He's hanging in there. The doctor has absolutely no idea how he's even still alive, I think that just about says it. But go and see him every so often. I don't have the time, and he always picks a fight with me.

Víctor Bagiardelli nodded. The next day, at lunchtime, he went by Old Man Giraudo's house. He found him arguing with the nurse.

Which one didn't lay? the old man was shouting.

I told you, the red one, answered the nurse.

Is she lame?

Not that I know of.

She doesn't have anything on her crest?

Anything like what?

An outbreak, some sore.

I'll take a look later.

Go now and bring her to me so I can check her.

Your son'll get angry.

There's no need for him to find out about it, Alicia. Bring her to me, and this stays between us.

The nurse looked at Víctor Bagiardelli, who had sat down on a bench by the edge of the bed. He nodded silently. As soon as the nurse had left the room, Víctor Bagiardelli took a pack of cigarettes out his trouser pocket and handed it to Old Man Giraudo, who hid it underneath his pillow.

So Miss Mahoney fell in love with you, and you rejected her right there on the plaza, said the old man then.

Who told you that?

When you're in the position I'm in you hear a lot of different things.

Did she say something?

Not a word. And she comes by every single night.

Víctor Bagiardelli went up to the window and stood

staring outside. From there you couldn't see the hill, just the yard, the earth where Old Man Giraudo had tended his garden, now overgrown with weeds that had been devastated by the cold. Towards the back, behind a little wall of privet, stood the chicken coop. After a while the nurse came out of it with a chicken clutched to her breast. The chicken's feet probed the air, as though seeking the ground.

Give her to me, said Old Man Giraudo when the nurse came into the room.

What is it, Coquita, why aren't you laying? he whispered sweetly to the chicken as his hand went quickly over and over her wings. He slid the edge of his nails between the plumage of her back and, forming a mound with his fingertips, palpated the moderate warmth of the down under her tail.

There's nothing wrong with you at all, he said at last. Why don't you take a look, Mr Engineer, since you don't need glasses. See if you can see anything out of the ordinary on her crest.

Víctor Bagiardelli approached and examined the tuft of fleshy, reddened little spikes.

Nothing out of the ordinary, he replied.

So Old Man Giraudo let go of the chicken, and, with some exertion, she straightened her feathers and sauntered out across the bed.

She'll shit on the bedspread, said the nurse. She had her arms crossed and was leaning against the doorframe.

Off you go, Alicia, said Old Man Giraudo. I'll let you know if I need anything.

The nurse spun around and walked out without another word. The chicken, meanwhile, rummaged around in the bedding until she found a breadcrumb forgotten from breakfast and gobbled it down in one peck.

How's the construction going? You making progress? asked Old Man Giraudo.

We've planted the lawn, said Víctor Bagiardelli. And the wall is almost finished. They'll be bringing in the trees in a couple of days. I got the oak. It's a majestic specimen, around twenty years old, with a trunk that's as thick as a lamppost, which at the height of my shoulders opens up into a fork. It's strong enough to withstand the transplant. They're going to take it out with the root ball and everything and wrap up its roots in plaster and burlap.

An oak! A twenty-year-old oak! Nothing more and nothing less than a twenty-year-old oak coming halfway across the country! I've already told you I'm not going to die, so there's no point in being in a rush. Just put in a little oak, any old little oak'll do fine.

But it's important, it has to have a real presence from the beginning, and provide shade and crown the whole ensemble.

Nonsense! Absolute nonsense! said Old Man Giraudo. Now: tell me a little bit about yourself. Do you like women?

Why do you ask that?

Because of Mahoney, needless to say. I can't understand why you didn't go to bed with her.

The hen had made a nest between the old man's feet and watched them from there with its big golden eyes, its neck stretched out slightly.

I don't have time for things like that, said Víctor Bagiardelli.

Everyone has time for things like that! She may be a little old to go riding, but she's still a terrific mount. But I guess you must know best. But you're not a queer, you say.

No.

You like women.

Yes.

Have you ever been married? Got any kids?

No.

Any type of family?

The chicken had pulled in its head now and, her wings at rest, was nestled in the old man's bedding.

I used to have my mum, said Víctor Bagiardelli. But she passed away a few years ago.

And your dad?

He died when I was young.

How young?

Sixteen.

You miss him?

Víctor Bagiardelli hesitated.

Not in general, he said. Or I just don't think about it. Sometimes – and this has been happening for a while now – certain smells remind me of him. As I've got older my sweat has changed so that it smells more like his. I notice it at night when I get into bed. That's where it catches me unawares and makes me think it's his smell that's there in the pillow.

Oh, well, everybody smells, said Old Man Giraudo.

Yeah, but this was his.

Hang on just a second because now I need to take a piss. It's the pills, they make me go all the time. Alicia! Urinal!

Alicia! Can you hear me? Urinal! Old Man Giraudo cried again, extending, like a skinny turtle, his neck towards the door.

The nurse got the portable urinal out from under the bed and with a swift and expert movement raised the covers and situated it between his legs, almost without altering the bedspread. For a second Víctor Bagiardelli glimpsed a big green and blue bruise towards the top of Giraudo's white thigh.

The hen followed this procedure with great interest but did not move, her neck only barely higher, her crest standing.

Old Man Giraudo shut his eyes and focused.

The nurse stood still, by his bedside, her arms crossed over her chest. Víctor Bagiardelli examined his cuticles, checked the length of his nails.

Below that silence rumbled the faint crystalline hum of an underground spring.

That's it, said Old Man Giraudo finally and sighed.

The nurse lifted the sheets, took out the portable urinal and left the room. They heard her emptying it in the bathroom and flushing the toilet.

As though summoned by that sound, the chicken stood up at the bottom of the bed and let out a long deep cluck that rose until it had become an unrestrained cackling.

There you go, she laid her egg, said Old Man Giraudo. Take it, our gift to you.

Víctor Bagiardelli left the house with the tentative warmth of the egg's shell cupped between his hands.

Soon, every seed of grass the town employees had scattered by the handful up and down the hill had transformed into a little mass of spiky blades sticking up out of the loose earth. It was still a sparse growth, but when from his desk in the middle of the street Víctor Bagiardelli raised his eyes to contemplate the hill, the leaves intermingled to the point that over and above the faded brown of the earth predominated the gleaming green of the newborn lawn. Before summer came, a couple of graves, or five, or six, or ten, would warp its immaculate sheen. For the moment, it was a magnificent hill. Higher up, on the embankment, they were starting to put the roof on the chapel, the wall was already done, the cemetery was taking shape. The time had come to dig the holes to plant in and Víctor Bagiardelli spent a week climbing the hill and returning, defying the wind with his big pages of sketches in his hands, unfurled. After him trailed one of the town's employees, carrying on his shoulder a bunch of stakes. With long, instinctive strides, Víctor Bagiardelli took stock of the terrain, and at each and every spot where a tree or shrub would grow he'd have a stake planted, and then he'd tie a red rag to its top. As he marked out the semicircle of willows, Víctor Bagiardelli remembered the grave in Almirante Costanzo where Miss Mahoney's mother lay, and he wondered whether he wasn't starting to repeat himself.

Maybe, he muttered, I rely too often on what I already know will work. Perhaps, as I've got older, Víctor Bagiardelli said to himself, I've lost my taste for risk, the adrenaline that comes with making a thing from scratch.

Past the town, the shadows of the clouds dashed out enormous fleeting splotches over the plain.

The employee trailing after him planted the last stake of the semicircle and stood staring at him.

Could I ask you a question? he said.

Víctor Bagiardelli nodded.

If you had some money saved and were thinking of buying a plot here, where would you say to get one?

For you, you mean? asked Víctor Bagiardelli and started across the hill. They still had to mark a little refuge with four maples and two plantain trees, on the other side.

For me and my family.

How many of you are there?

My wife and me, and three kids, the oldest twelve, a boy, the youngest five, a girl.

These days everybody wants to get their hands on

the highest ground, and the lower land gets sold for cheap, said Víctor Bagiardelli. I'd recommend two plots together, at a slight remove from the entrance gate, but not too far. One for you and one for your children. If they want to sell it tomorrow, and find themselves some new location, they will find a buyer. When these trees have tops that area will really be very attractive, and the prices will go up. If you end up selling, you'll triple your investment.

So low ground, said the employee.

As close as you can get to where we marked the little hill of casuarinas, poplars and sweetgum. It's a combo that never fails. Bright in the summer, richly coloured in the autumn, and in the winter the casuarinas keep things interesting, too. In any season it will be a beautiful spot for your bereaved to come and visit you. The harmony of the colours, the sound of the foliage in the wind, the beauty of the design will attenuate the pain of your loved ones.

On low ground it will be, then! said the municipal employee, barely able to contain his excitement. Thanks for the advice!

Oh, it's no trouble, said Víctor Bagiardelli. Then he paused and for a moment just contemplated the hill, the town, the blotches of shadow over the plain, the distant horizon, sending out its clouds. The wind made the red material flutter ablaze around the stakes.

Otherwise, said Víctor Bagiardelli, his gaze planted on the horizon, buy by the semicircle of willows. The area around the semicircle will also be worth a lot, he said. It's sort of my signature.

That afternoon, Víctor Bagiardelli did not go for a walk in the countryside. He stationed himself in front of Old Man Giraudo's house and waited. The neighbour opposite had mean dogs that started to bark. When she saw who it was, the neighbour invited him in, so he wouldn't have to stand outside, with that freezing wind.

I'm alright here, said Víctor Bagiardelli and sank his face into its padding of scarf.

Through the fence the dogs sniffed his shoes.

The neighbour offered him hot coffee. Víctor Bagiardelli declined again. Finally the neighbour went back inside and the dogs calmed down. Almost immediately sunset started over the mountains and the first streetlamps came on. Víctor Bagiardelli saw the night nurse arriving, wrapped up in a great wool shawl. A moment later, the afternoon nurse left, buttoning up her jacket, her head covered with a knotted kerchief. Five minutes later it was Miss Mahoney who left, and, with her hands plunged into the pockets of her blazer, she set off walking down the pavement. Hidden in the shadows, Víctor Bagiardelli waited until she reached the corner. Only then did he cross the street and run after her, to track her at a decent remove. He leaped from shadow to shadow and trunk to trunk. He got the benefit of the scarcity of streetlamps, which lit the town only at the crossings and in front of the most important buildings. With feline instinct he evaded the heaps of dry leaves that the residents would sweep and leave in the gutter, waiting for a dry day to offer them up to the fire. Miss Mahoney finally got to her house, a simple little place: a door, two windows. Víctor Bagiardelli saw a lamp switch on behind the curtains, hanging from the ceiling like a shining fig. And behind the yellow creaminess of the veiled light, the cemetery designer gleaned Miss Mahoney's shadow. She heated up a bowl of soup and ate it sitting by herself at the table, blowing each time on the spoon before sipping it delicately.

She was reaching the midway point of her dinner when Víctor Bagiardelli took a deep breath and walked up to the door. He took off his gloves, raised his arm and made a fist with his right hand. He was on the verge of knocking, but at the last moment he hesitated. He paused, he thought it over again, he took a few steps back, then quickly returned.

Mr Bagiardelli, she said when she opened the door. She looked surprised, but most of all, disturbed. He was there, with his gloves in his hands.

Do you need something? she asked, suddenly tough, putting distance between them.

Yes, he said.

What?

Víctor Bagiardelli's lips began to draw words in one direction, but right away they turned back on themselves, jumbling up.

What? Miss Mahoney asked again.

The gate, he said, at last.

The rest just poured out.

I can't work like this... he won't let me see it... the mayor has to talk to him... under these conditions I can't be held responsible for the way things end up... I've never been in this situation before... someone like me, you know... my level... fighting with a village blacksmith... if my colleagues find out... it's outrageous! It's an outrage... I need to know what he's doing. Right now! I demand to know!

Shielded by the door, Miss Mahoney nodded.

I'll talk to the mayor tomorrow, she said. Anything else?

No, that was it, said Víctor Bagiardelli and stalked off.

They transplanted poplars and ash trees bare root. They unwrapped their stems from the damp sackcloth in which they had arrived and rested them at the bottom of the holes the town's employees had so meticulously dug. Afterwards, they filled up the cavities with fertilised soil and watered them with water from the tanker. Meanwhile the plantains on the central path, the cypresses, the casuarinas, the damson and ornamental plums, the gingko bilobas that would yellow up the gorge, they planted with their root balls and all, exactly as the nurseries had sent them. For the time being they were no more than sickly little trees tied to their stakes, just branches with hibernating buds, sleeping through their latencies. As soon as the cold released its hold and the roots discovered their new liberty, they would untangle and start to extend into the fertile earth, down, down, until they found the centre of the hill. Their stems would swell on the surface and their branches would be covered with new leaves. By the time spring was over the shapes that Víctor Bagiardelli had imagined on his own would enrapture the inhabitants of Colonel Isabeta. And so, for years and years, as the trees grew to their maximum size and attained their ideal shape, as the colours of their foliage changed with the seasons, while always, in any month, just exactly as he had planned for it to happen, there would be some bush flowering, and summer after summer the fragrances of fresh pollen would inundate the whole. Every time a resident of Colonel Isabeta died and the cortège transported the body to the cemetery, the trees Víctor Bagiardelli had chosen would bend their branches to comfort the mourners in their distress.

The wind of the plain, on the grey day covered in winter, made the flimsy, newly planted saplings vibrate, and from his desk in the street Víctor Bagiardelli imagined what this place would look like once he had left it. The chapel, above, looked as though it had appeared out of a fairytale. The grass was strong and proliferating, fluffing up the hill, its roots extending rapidly. The ossuary, in the ravine, was discreet, just a marble cross, a metallic door that led into the vault and two concrete angels, but tasteful, the entrance's custodians. In the departed children's rose garden the thorny stems were already getting longer, and the design the plants' placement drew between the paths of split brick could be surmised without effort. In a few weeks they could expect the first white buds.

The cemetery was finished. All that remained was the entrance gate and the oak, up at the very top.

Two days later, the blacksmith delivered the entrance gate. They brought it up in the little van, the two wings on top, one over the other. It took five men to take them down. The hinges weren't yet ready, so they just leaned them up against the pillars to see how it would look. The gate was magnificent. The blacksmith had stayed faithful to the design down to the tiniest detail. The figure eights of the frieze were brutal and definitive. The tension of the metal immediately surpassed them, and the thick bars went upwards, thinning and lightening until almost evanescing against the sky. And in the centre, in the circle made when the two wings came together, and where the lock and the bolt were fitted, the letters: the C of Colonel and the I of Isabeta, inclined slightly forward, with their flourishes and tendrils elegantly brushing one another.

Víctor Bagiardelli's eyes shone with tears of excitement.

I owe you an apology, he said to the blacksmith as he offered his hand. It's a real work of art.

It turned out pretty good, didn't it? The top part gave me some trouble, but it turned out alright.

It's beautiful, said Víctor Bagiardelli.

We'll drop off an invoice at the Town Hall tomorrow, said the blacksmith's wife, peeking out from behind him.

That afternoon, Víctor Bagiardelli went to see Old Man Giraudo. He found him yawning with his head buried in his pillows. The light of the siesta hour came through the window, fell over the blankets on the bed and warmed up the air somewhat.

Were you asleep? asked Víctor Bagiardelli.

I was thinking on some things, that's all, said the old man and rubbed his eyes with his fingertips.

They brought the gate today, Víctor Bagiardelli told him. It's an incredible gate. Now all we need is the oak.

The oak, sighed Old Man Giraudo.

Yes.

You'll plant the oak and be done?

Yes, sir.

Are you happy?

Víctor Bagiardelli nodded.

Very much so, he said. I promised your son I would do my very best, and with the oak up at the top, this is going to be the best cemetery of my entire career. I can't say it was all my doing, the land is ideal, it just needed someone to understand it. I can assure you there is no lovelier place where you could be buried.

Old Man Giraudo's lips drew a polite smile. His eyes still looked lost in half-sleep.

Would you like to go and see it? asked Víctor Bagiardelli.

Heavens no, I don't like to leave the house, thank you all the same. The last few times I didn't know a soul on the street. Everyone worth knowing has died by now. I'd rather just stay here and remember them in peace.

We could get you a wheelchair, or a stretcher. Something that wouldn't upset your hip.

I'd rather you get me a wheelchair so I could go and see about my garden or visit my chickens, not to see some cemetery.

It's a beautiful place, I know you'd like it. The buds on the cherry trees are swelling and will bloom in a few days. And you could get to see the chapel and take a look at the blacksmith's gate. Miss Mahoney will be there. We can even get you a cigarette. Picture that, smoking a cigarette while all around you all those new little trees sprout up and gleam green.

Old Man Giraudo shrugged, as though in apology.

I appreciate your good intentions, he said, but no thank you. I'd rather not see it.

I understand, said Víctor Bagiardelli. Forgive me, I may have been overly enthusiastic.

I can sympathise, said Old Man Giraudo. But keep this poor old man entertained a little while longer, tell me about what you're planning to do now that you've finished this job.

I haven't finished it yet, there's still the oak.

And when the oak arrives? What will you do then?

I guess I'll rest. This cemetery is my masterwork. All the magazines will come and take pictures of it, I can promise you that.

It'll open many doors for you, I imagine.

I'm sure it will.

Old Man Giraudo smiled wistfully, or maybe sympathetically.

How old are you? he asked.

Forty-five.

You're in the prime of your life, said Old Man Giraudo. And you've got so much left ahead of you.

His voice got thinner as he spoke.

So much left to live, Old Man Giraudo repeated and sighed.

Then he closed his eyes.

I'm tired, he said. This siesta sun puts me to sleep, I'd like to rest a while.

Of course, I'm so sorry to have bothered you, said Víctor Bagiardelli and rose from his chair.

It's never a bother. Thank you for coming, said Old Man Giraudo.

Víctor Bagiardelli nodded.

Goodbye, he said, resting both hands on the edge of the bed.

Old Man Giraudo barely tensed his eyelids.

See you, he muttered.

The golden dust of afternoon hovered all around him.

All night the wind blew over Colonel Isabeta, but it failed to disturb in any way the dreams cradling Víctor Bagiardelli, a man both exhausted and satisfied. When he woke up he was still immersed in shadow. It was the milky darkness at the crack of dawn in winter: from the kitchen came the crash of Elvita's pots and pans and the low buzz of the newsreader on the radio, but outside it was still night. Víctor Bagiardelli shut his eyes and swore to himself he would only sleep for five more minutes. He let himself drift off into a blank sleep until, suddenly, a decisive hand shook his shoulder.

Víctor! Víctor! someone was whispering with urgency.

The first light of day was beating down on the shutters.

You could make out now the outline of the furniture in the room. The mirror was a splotch of tenuous light.

Víctor! insisted the voice.

His mouth was sticky, his hair greasy. His smell, which had permeated the lukewarm sheets, enveloped him like a cocoon.

Víctor, it's important, insisted Miss Mahoney for the third time.

So then he did sit up and see her there, sitting on the edge of his bed, like an apparition. Miss Mahoney was forcing a cold look, and he noticed, right away.

The oak! he said then. Did something happen to the oak? Did they say it would be here any minute? he said and leaped out of bed.

The big hole was ready now at the top of the hill. It was as wide as a vehicle, and if a person fell into it, he'd need a ladder to be able to climb out.

Get dressed, said Miss Mahoney. The mayor needs to see you right away.

They ran across the plaza, Miss Mahoney in the lead, her hands pressed against the sides of her coat to keep the wind from blowing them up. Víctor Bagiardelli behind her, not knowing exactly what he was running for.

Is there some problem? he asked.

Yes, said Miss Mahoney.

They went into the Town Hall, and Víctor Bagiardelli saw two men in glasses leaning over a desk. They were consulting a pile of thick books. With their fingertips they were following the tiny lines. Councilman Romero was seated alone, at a different desk, with his arms crossed over his chest. There was nothing on his desk, not even a cup of coffee. Miss Mahoney kept going, straight to the mayor's office.

They've filed for an injunction, said Giraudo when he saw them come in.

Víctor Bagiardelli looked at him uncomprehendingly.

It's the oak, said the mayor. Where'd you get the oak?

I bought it.

From whom?

A couple, they were selling the trees from their yard. A colleague tipped me off about it.

The price was leaked, and Romero started saying we had inflated the budget, said the mayor. And to be honest with you, looking at the numbers, it is insane to pay that much for a plant.

It's a good oak, it's almost twenty years old, that's what it costs, said Víctor Bagiardelli. It's essential that the oak is fully grown and powerful to look at from the start. It's the focal point of the whole composition. What draws everybody's eye.

Well, he's also threatening to file an official complaint against me for embezzlement and another against you for fraud.

But that's ridiculous.

Don't worry, said the mayor. I know you're not guilty, that you acted according to the letter of the law. I've got three lawyers working on it. But we're going to have to get rid of the oak.

Impossible! said Víctor Bagiardelli.

The mayor stood up behind his desk.

Listen here, he said. This municipality cannot and will not provide such funds for a tree. Still less so for its cost of transportation. I don't know what was going through your head when you came up with the idea that we could cover something like this. So call it all off, and we are not going to discuss it any further here.

But the hole is there already.

So fill it.

But without the oak the whole composition's thrown off.

The mayor was tired. He slumped into his chair and placed his hands on his temples.

I'm sure you don't need the oak, he said. The cemetery is already fantastic, you've done a great job.

But you don't understand...

Oh I understand perfectly, friend, the mayor raised his voice again. But it's a little hot to saunter into the kitchen just now. Romero won't relent, and he's threatening to start a popular uprising against us. He says we reserved the best lots for municipal employees, that other people's dead get lesser treatment.

That's not true.

It's not true, but all our employees have been buying where you told them to: near the entrance gate, near the semicircle of willows. And on top of that my father has taken it into his head that if he ever dies he does not wish to be buried in this cemetery. He's let half the town know by now, he even wrote a letter to the radio, for them to read on the air. His last wish is to be buried in Deheza.

That can't be.

Oh it can, said the mayor. With my father, anything can be.

Víctor Bagiardelli went into the house without ringing the bell. He did not greet the nurse, whom he left staring after him as he stormed down the hallway.

It was you! You gave him the idea! he shrieked, full of fury, pointing his finger at him.

His voice was trembling. The veins in his neck were all bulging.

You told him the price of the oak! You suggested the injunction! he said. Romero doesn't have the sense to plan a thing like this.

Old Man Giraudo smiled from ear to ear.

Good morning, come in, come in, make yourself comfortable. What kind of greeting is this, Engineer? Where have all your manners gone?

And on top of everything now you want to be buried in Deheza!

Either way there's no point in digging my spot up just yet. I've already explained to you that I have no intention of dying.

You are over a hundred years old! You've got to...

Careful, Engineer! Respect! Old Man Giraudo stopped him. His breakfast tray was resting on his lap. Now tell me, would you like some tea, or coffee? What can the nurse get you? As you can see, I am enjoying my morning mate brew. Alicia! Alicia! Let's see if we can get her at least to offer a seat to this young man.

You are a deplorable human being, said Víctor Bagiardelli.

Ah, the pleasures of living well! said Old Man Giraudo and dropped a small piece of toast into his mug. Nothing better than being insulted while one dunks a piece of bread in one's favourite infusion, he said. His hand was not trembling. He rescued the toast with his teaspoon and ferried it into his mouth. As his naked gums undid the wet crumbs, Old Man Giraudo cleaned off his chin with a napkin and closed his eyes for a moment, savouring the taste of bread dipped in brewed mate. He sighed, and his bliss was visible in his face.

Some things never change, he said.

Víctor Bagiardelli couldn't stand it anymore. He turned and walked out.

See you around, Engineer! See you! he heard Old Man Giraudo yelling from his bed as he made his way down the hallway.

Come back next year and see if we let you plant your tree!

That afternoon, instead of walking through the countryside towards the horizon, Víctor Bagiardelli went to the cemetery, which was nearly complete. He stopped where he always set up his portable desk and stayed looking at the hill. Up above, at the top, what was absent could not help but be noticed: a naked bench, defenceless. A masterwork that lacked its triumphant finish.

The perfect cemetery had turned into a disaster.

I thought I'd find you here, Miss Mahoney interrupted his thoughts. And I thought you might be in need of some company.

The aesthetic balance of the composition has been destroyed completely, said Víctor Bagiardelli. The lack of an oak breaches the harmony of the whole. The vanishing lines lead nowhere. You understand. I'm sure you can see what I'm saying.

I can, but it's not that bad, said Miss Mahoney.

It's a disaster, said Víctor Bagiardelli. It could have been perfect, and it's a disaster.

Don't be so hard on yourself, it's a beautiful cemetery, said Miss Mahoney. And up top we can put in another little tree of some sort. As the years go by, it'll grow and pick up volume.

It's not the same, said Víctor Bagiardelli.

Come on, let's take a little walk. Stop thinking about it, said Miss Mahoney and patted his back.

The wind of the previous evening had completely cleared the grey and stormy clouds that had covered the sky for days. Now the sun was setting neatly over Colonel Isabeta. It wasn't so cold anymore. Spring would arrive any day now.

Víctor Bagiardelli and Miss Mahoney walked next to one another down the middle of the street, their backs to the hill, moving away from the cemetery. There was almost no space between the edges of their shoulders.

Their hands on the verge of touching, without having done so just yet.

Is it true there's no woman expecting you elsewhere? asked Miss Mahoney.

No, there's no one, said Víctor Bagiardelli. Just the cemeteries. I don't know how to do anything else.

Do you have other jobs?

I always have other jobs. They want a lawn cemetery in Tapalcán. Another one in General Cabrera.

That's a long way from here.

Yes, it's far, said Víctor Bagiardelli. And for next year I've signed on for something in Chaco, and another one, near Paraná. But they're routine commissions, no terrain as promising as this one was.

You are brilliant, said Miss Mahoney. I'm sure you'll come up with something soon.

Their walk had taken them to the block where her house was. There they were, in front of them, the door and the two windows behind which Miss Mahoney's days were spent.

Would you like to come in? she asked. Her pupils trembled under the light of the streetlamp.

I have to get up early tomorrow, said Víctor Bagiardelli. Make calls to wrap up the return of the oak tree, make sure they get the hinges on the gate, meet with the lawyers, make sure they water the agapanthus.

Would you like to come in? Miss Mahoney asked again, without lowering her eyes.

Víctor Bagiardelli smiled sadly.

Alright, he said. Just for a little while.

FOREST LIFE

Dad, are you almost done? asked Mabel, sitting on the boards on the porch, her feet hanging outwards on the other side of the railing, her hair loose and wavy, cascading down.

Old Wutrich said nothing in reply. Squatting down beside her, he was cutting one by one the little flowers from a branch he'd fetched himself. He took them by their little stems and linked them together in among his daughter's curls, trying to set them over the sections where her hair was greyer.

In front of the house, down the hill, the hard sun of the autumn siesta was paling the gleam of the pine trees that extended over the land and the mountains.

Are you almost done? Mabel asked again.

One more, said Wutrich, biting his lip. His fingers were shaking. The flowers were too fragile. He slid a strand of hair in around the petals of a zinnia until he could be sure that it would stay. Then he stood. He took two steps back, looked at her from this side, then the other. Flowers in Mabel's hair like a shower of confetti. The light blue and red of the baby verbenas, Queen Anne's lace like snowflakes, barely violet cupflowers, fuchsia spikes off eryngium buds.

Like your mother used to fix you up, said Wutrich. I've just got to fill in a little more, up front.

No, sir, that's enough, said Mabel, and the flowers scattered over the cloud of her hair.

Let's get going, it's getting late, she said and went inside for her jacket.

They went down the way that cut straight through the pine forest, following the downward slope and then the path through the ravine. The wind was playing in the pine branches, but above, in the highest sections; beneath their intertwining crowns, all was calm. Only a few rays of sun managed to pierce through the bower. They lit up the dry dust that was floating in the air, drawing dazzling white circles over the foliage. From time to time old Wutrich would rest by leaning against some stone or other. Mabel would wait for him with her arms crossed, the heels of her shoes sinking into the thick layer of densely packed needles.

Let's go, Dad, hurry up, it's getting late, she would insist after a while.

Yes, yes, let's get going.

They rounded the high hill, close to where the springs came together, and before them appeared the bare slope, just stripped branches that were starting to dry. And in the distance, at the limit of what was still the forest, along the wall of brown trunks, the lumberjacks bustling about like ants. Their yellow helmets were little nervous points heaped at the base of a tall pine. They came and went around the base of it, until, after some time, with a slow crash, the pine came down.

Hurry, Dad, hurry, Mabel said when it did, and they kept on walking.

They went into the town by the road that led in from the ford and headed straight for the funeral home. All the windows were shut. They rang the bell, and nobody answered. They banged on the door to the street.

The hearse is here, so Moro can't have gone too far, said Wutrich.

They kept banging the door until they heard the sounds of something opening inside.

Open up, it's me, Wutrich, shouted the old man.

Who died? asked the voice on the other side.

Nobody, nobody died.

Then what do you want?

Just to tell you something.

Mabel took a deep breath and straightened her posture. She smoothed the flap of her jacket, pinched her cheeks, made sure the flowers hadn't fallen out of her hair.

Moro Scarafia came out onto the pavement buttoning his suit jacket. He was barefoot, but he still had the suit on, with bowtie and waistcoat and all. He was very tall and very slim, and his beard made a grey crescent below his white chin.

What is it? he asked.

I've come to offer her, said Wutrich, signalling Mabel. Your daughter?

She knows how to sew, and she can make a good dinner, and she can clean, said Wutrich. You're a good man, you're old enough. You can't stay like this your whole life. She's already taken care of me, she's experienced.

Moro scratched his beard. He squinted with one eye. He squinted with the other.

What about you? he said.

I come with her.

Moro thought for a while. Mabel looked at his hands, his long, pale fingers, the dark hair around his knuckles.

Is she able to breed? asked Moro.

Wutrich looked at Mabel.

Mabel looked down.

Should still be, said Mabel.

Moro scratched at one eyebrow, nibbled at a nail, scratched behind an ear.

Is it that they're kicking you out from up there? he asked.

Yes sir, Wutrich nodded.

Moro didn't say anything. He went back to scratching.

I guess not, he said at last.

At Bronzino's place there were the same old folks as always, and the television installed on top of the column, the coffee machine, the yellow walls, the trophies covered in dirt on the shelves.

When Wutrich opened the door, they all turned around to look at him. He acted like he didn't notice. He went along with his daughter up to a table and helped her take off her jacket. Her green dress lit up the smoke in the air. She had sewn it herself, with her own hands, sitting under the pines, in the endless afternoons of their last summer. Around the edge of the camisole and in the little flaps along the neckline you could see the neat, extremely tight, even stitches.

Old Wutrich went up to the counter and ordered a Coca-Cola and a gin. Bronzino served him the helping of gin.

You go on, I'll bring you your Coke, he said and vanished into the back.

Wutrich nodded, but he didn't go back to where Mabel was. He walked up to the table where the lawyer Kovach was drinking coffee with the head of the generating station. He sat down between them and raised his glass.

Cheers, he said.

Cheers, the lawyer Kovach and the head of the generating station answered him in unison. Like everyone in the town, they knew old Wutrich, but from a distance.

I'm giving her away, said Wutrich indicating Mabel. She knows how to sew, that dress she's wearing she made herself. She cooks. She's clean. She's willing. She learns fast.

Why should anyone want her? asked Kovach.

Old Wutrich shrugged. She'll be a good wife.

The head of the generating station burst out laughing. Are you serious? he said.

The men at the other tables didn't even try to pretend they weren't listening. Mabel was listening, too. Some of the little flowers had come untangled from her hair and fallen onto the Formica of the table. She ground them with her fingers.

So I guess you're not interested, said Wutrich.

Kovach shook his head no.

Wutrich took his glass, stood up and went over to the next table.

What about you all? he asked. Anybody want her? She was raised up on the hill, but she's a good woman. Better than any of them from down here.

The men thanked him and said no. One of them almost let out a laugh, but the others elbowed him in time, and he kept quiet.

Wutrich went to the next table. He was on the verge of starting to speak when Mabel took him by the arm.

Let's go, Dad, she said. It's not worth it.

But...

Let's go, Dad, come on.

They left by way of the street with the shops on it and took a narrow path up, a shortcut that took them directly to the pines without them having to cross the river. They didn't talk. Mabel up ahead, her steps quick and firm, her lips tight. From time to time she would sigh and stop to wait for her old man, who was walking slower.

Tomorrow you can come in the blue dress, said Wutrich once they were already walking on the dry foliage. The pine trunks creaked in the wind.

Quiet, Dad, said Mabel.

Else we can take out some money on loan, and I'll get you a new fabric.

Mabel didn't answer. She put a hand on her stomach and threw up over a bunch of dead mushrooms. Her hair fell forward and covered her face. Old Wutrich moved off and looked the other way.

Mabel wiped her mouth with the edge of her dress.

No one wears flowers in their hair, she said. I don't know why I listened to you.

Her quick fingers unravelled one by one the petals from her hair.

Soon it would be night. The dust suspended between the trunks was still. It looked like fog, but it was dry.

Hurry up, Dad, said Mabel. I didn't bring the torch.

After the second valley, the path narrowed even more, and to get to the road you had to climb up over the stones. They reached it as the sun was burying itself behind the hills. Mabel got up on the guardrail and looked out at the pine trees undulating at her feet, covering the mountains like a blanket. In the ravines, shadow zones formed where everything was already dark blue, almost violet. The last rays of sun hit the crowns of the pines that grew over the peaks and dyed them orange.

Mabel sat on a stone and waited for her father to catch his breath. Around them the heat of the day was going out of the trunks, which were creaking, dry. They'd left the town on the other side of the mountains, and from there they couldn't even see it, but the wind brought in the smell of the smoke of its chimneys, and, from time to time, the bark of some dog. It also brought another sound, the noise of an engine, which showed itself and vanished between the dips in the road.

It's not a truck, said Wutrich.

It's coming up the road, said Mabel. Is it a four-by-four?

Wutrich shook his head.

It's coming fast, it must be a motorcycle, he said.

Yes, said Mabel.

After a while, they saw the lashes of light coming down the side of the next hill over. A motocross cycle was zigzagging in between the pines, its roar louder and louder. It was already almost completely dark when it showed up in the curve and lit up the interiors of their eyes. The driver braked next to them and turned off the engine. A white leather suit covered his body from head to toe. On his chest and his legs were painted ads for oil and spare car parts. He took off his helmet without getting off his bike. He lit a cigarette, and in the glow of the lighter Mabel was able to distinguish his face. He was a young man, with long hair.

Nobody's going to want her here, he said after a first drag.

Mabel and Wutrich looked at him without fully understanding.

Your daughter, said the driver of the motorcycle and pointed to Mabel. In the town they're not going to want her, but I know a place where you might get some interest.

What place? asked Mabel.

Right up by the reservoir, out by the dam, closer to the city.

Who would be interested? asked Mabel.

There are Japanese there, said the driver of the motorcycle, who took a second drag.

No way I'm going with a Japanese, said Mabel.

They've got money, said the boy. A lot.

Ah, the Japanese with the greenhouses, murmured Mabel.

Those are the ones, said the boy. I know one who's been looking for a woman. I'll take you to him for a fee.

Do they really have money? Wutrich wanted to know.

Yes, said the boy and brought the cigarette back to his lips.

Mabel thought about it for a second.

No, she said after. I would never be with a Japanese.

Then there's nothing for me to do here, said the boy on the motorcycle. Let me know if you change your mind.

She's obstinate, she won't change it, said Wutrich. When she says no, there's no sense in trying to force her.

Alright, that's fine, said the boy on the motorcycle.

Then he flattened the cigarette into the road, backed up his bike and took off downhill.

That night they had stones thrown at them. They were roused by the thuds on the roof of the cabin. Mabel looked at the clock: it was past midnight.

It's the lumberjacks, said Wutrich.

No, said Mabel and grabbed the shotgun. She opened the door to the porch and shot into the air.

When the rumble of it fell quiet among the pines, she could make out the laughs and the whispers.

Wild old woman, they shouted at her.

If it's some dick you want, come with us, we'll give it to you.

They were the voices of young boys, kids. Someone must have told them what had happened at the bar.

Mabel reloaded and fired again.

They're from town, she explained to Wutrich. The stupid kids from town. They must have come up on their bicycles.

Get out of here, she shouted into the darkness. Go away, she shouted. Out.

One week later, once the noise of the chainsaws was sounding too close, and the men from the pine forest were threatening to call the police to get them out of there, the boy with the motorcycle came back.

He came back in a blue truck driven by a Japanese man. They parked out in front, the boy with the motorcycle got out, and the Japanese man stayed sitting behind the wheel, staring into the windscreen, without looking up at the cabin. The boy with the motorcycle clapped his hands. Mabel had already heard them, but anyway she waited a while before going out onto the porch. Wutrich followed.

What's going on? asked Mabel, shielding her eyes with her arm.

I brought the Japanese guy, said the boy.

I told you I didn't want anything to do with that, answered Mabel.

They're going to burn down your house. If you don't go, they're going to burn it down. They're getting close, said the boy with the motorcycle. They've already logged up to where the springs came together and now they're coming this way.

Mabel didn't say anything.

He has money? asked old Wutrich, peeking out from behind her.

Yes, sir, said the boy with the motorcycle.

Tell him to get out, said old Wutrich and then went inside.

Mabel tucked her hair behind her ears and shooed away the chickens that were milling around among the boards on the porch.

Can he understand everything? she asked the boy then.

He can, he speaks good Spanish, he's one of the only ones.

Mabel took off her apron and laid it over a stump. The Japanese man was waiting for her with his hands in his pockets, leaning against the fender of the truck. He was short, petit, with short hair that was very dark with gel in it, combed to the right. He was wearing jeans and a beige jacket with patches on the elbows that was a little bit too small for him. He looked like he was about Mabel's age, or slightly younger.

Mabel gestured to him, and the Japanese man followed her. They went into the forest. The Japanese man walked without taking his hands out of his pockets. The boy with the motorcycle stayed where he was, by the house, watching Mabel and the Japanese man talking in among the pines. At one point the Japanese man reached out and stroked Mabel's hair. Then she climbed up the slope.

He'll pay you your whole fee, that's what we agreed on, she told the boy with the motorcycle.

Old Wutrich was spying on them through the window.

Come out, Dad, Mabel called to him. This is Sakoiti. Come out so I can introduce you.

The next day, Mabel killed all the chickens, put them in two burlap sacks and went down to sell them in the town. Moro Scarafia was sitting on the little wall of the funeral home and waved at her, but she kept her eyes on the other side and acted like she didn't see him. When she came out of the butcher's she found Moro waiting for her there in front.

So you guys are leaving, he said.

Yes, said Mabel.

Have they logged a lot already?

They're moving pretty quickly, said Mabel. They're in a hurry because they're paying them per tree.

Who's doing the logging?

Outsiders, with chainsaws.

Yeah, you can hear them from here, said Moro Scarafia. If the wind comes in this direction, you can hear them.

They never stop, they've been logging day and night, said Mabel.

Yeah, said Moro Scarafia. Then he fell silent.

Well, I'll be going, said Mabel.

Sure, you'll have plenty to do. I've had a month and a half here with nothing happening, said Moro Scarafia, gesturing towards the funeral home. Not that I wish anybody ill, but I'm awfully bored.

Didn't they say Lucra's widow was done for? asked Mabel.

They might be doing her wake in San Aldo, though, they have a vault up there.

Oh, I didn't know that, said Mabel.

Her husband's up there, said Moro, and from the pocket of his shirt he took out a pack of cigarettes and offered her one.

No, thanks, I don't smoke.

So, said Moro Scarafia then, Japanese.

Yeah, Mabel smiled and looked down.

Is your dad happy?

He'll be fine. He will be fine.

I kept thinking about it afterwards, the other day, said Moro. I didn't know what to do, you caught me by surprise, I didn't know what to say. We've never talked that much, you and me. I barely know you, I've just seen you around.

That's fine, you were fine, she said. Cordial and correct. Don't you worry.

I'm not worried, but I kept on thinking about how things might have gone. Your dad comes up with all kinds of ideas.

It was my idea, said Mabel.

Moro looked her in the eye for a second, then quickly looked down.

It's empty inside, he said. If you like, you can come in and help me a while. I have everything in there, my bed, my coffee. It's comfortable, I'm sure we can find something to do...

Now? she asked.

If you like.

Sure, OK, said Mabel. Yeah, she said, that would be fine.

On the day they had agreed on for their departure, Sakoiti arrived on time, very early in the morning. In his hand he had five carnations, two red and three white, wrapped up in a cone of slick brown paper.

They're mine, he explained to Mabel, as he was handing them to her. These are the ones I grow. In my valley they all have roses, I'm the only one who does carnations. The others sell a lot for Mother's Day, for Valentine's Day; carnations, on the other hand, are more of a constant, they bloom all year long.

Sure, I see, I see, said Mabel, who didn't know what to do with the flowers.

Then she loaded the suitcases into the back of the truck and called to old Wutrich, who was walking around among the pines behind the house, stroking their bark.

Come on, Dad, she said. It's time.

Sakoiti started the engine, and they headed down between the trees, Mabel sitting in the middle, old Wutrich leaning against the window.

When they had cleared the first slope and rounded the hill, the view opened up and showed them all the mountains, the valley below, just tree stumps and strewn branches, all the way to the town.

Shut your eyes, Dad, I don't want you seeing, said Mabel, but old Wutrich didn't seem to hear her.

Shut your eyes! Mabel shouted then, and with the palm of her hand she blocked his view.

Yes, yes, fine, murmured old Wutrich and squeezed his eyelids tight.

They travelled for hours, the sun arching over the hood of the truck. Around noon they ate some sandwiches that Mabel had made. Then old Wutrich rested his head against the windowpane and slept. When he woke up, they were driving down a straight highway, in the middle of a plain. To the sides you saw a sea of low weeds.

Where are we? Are we far from the reservoir? asked Wutrich.

Do you need to go to the bathroom? Mabel said.

Yes.

They stopped, and old Wutrich urinated, sheltered by the truck.

Before him, in the distance, the horizon reverberated with an almost imperceptible outline. It might be mountains, but they were very remote, or it could be the suggestion of a storm.

Mabel got out, too, to stretch her legs. The wind blew up her hair, and she rushed to gather it back with both hands. When she looked up she saw Sakoiti standing in front of her.

What are you looking at? Mabel asked him.

You are very pretty, said Sakoiti, immediately looking down.

Then, along the edge of the road, rusty billboards started up advertising snacks and by-the-hour motels. Gradually they saw a few houses scattered out over the plain. They passed by some barns, a petrol station, very long light simple walls skirting the ditch, a wooden gate and, alongside it, a line of poplars.

Here we are, Sakoiti finally said and slowed down. He turned off onto a road that was narrow but paved that led up to a massive iron gate. Beside the gate there was a guard and a security booth. Sakoiti said his name, the guard looked for it on his list and let them through. The greenery started as soon as they went through the gate. Inside, the road went through light rises of gleaming grass, groupings of ornamental laurels and some plane-trees. Further in there was a pink mansion, with a portico, columns and many rows of windows.

A hefty woman, stuffed into a yellow suit, came out to receive them.

Señor Sakoiti, how wonderful to have you back again. And you all must be Señor Wutrich and his daughter, pleasure to meet you, I'm Señora Mónica, she said as she shook everyone's hands and gave them each a card with her name on it.

Old Wutrich looked at both sides of the card.

The woman's name was Mónica Adriana Ballegra, and she was the director of the Good Rest nursing home.

It's a care home, said old Wutrich.

Yes, Dad, Mabel said to him. You'll be fine.

Of course, of course, said Señora Mónica. Come and let me give you a guided tour.

She showed them the miniature cinema and the dance hall, the regular dining room, the porch that got sun all afternoon. She showed them the lounge chairs, a gazebo for playing cards, the heated pool. She showed them the infirmary and the art therapy room, the administrative offices, the booths where they could receive telephone calls.

Everything is designed for a wonderful rest, said Señora Mónica as they went down a long hallway.

She stopped in front of a room, looked for a key and opened the door. The room was spacious, the windows were covered with white curtains. Fixed to the wall, in front of the bed, there was a giant television.

The buttons on the remote control are also extra large, said Señora Mónica.

Old Wutrich picked up the remote control. Every button was the size of a die and springy and soft.

Señora Mónica showed them the bathroom covered in decorative tiles, the metal rails by the toilet and the shower, and the red cord that would summon the nurses if anyone slipped.

The best place, said Sakoiti. It's what I'd promised you.

How are you going to pay for all this? asked Mabel.

It's been paid for, said Señora Mónica. Señor Sakoiti has covered a full year already, in advance.

Mabel nodded and said nothing.

Old Wutrich opened the door to the wardrobe and looked at the shelves. He sat down on the bed, trying out the mattress, feeling the pillow.

Child, are you sure? he asked.

Yes, Dad. You'll stay here, said Mabel.

I haven't shown you the kitchen or the covered gym, said Señora Mónica.

That's fine, said Mabel. There's no need.

In the valley where the plant nurseries were there lived eight Japanese families, spaced out, one after the next, along a sandy road that followed the bed of a dry river. Around each house there were three or four greenhouses, a shed made of sheet metal and some dogs. Sakoiti's house was the last, at the end of the road, where the valley narrowed to its end.

Now, here we are, said Sakoiti when they pulled up.

Mabel nodded, her eyes getting lost in that ground without a single tree.

Inflating and deflating with the wind, the plastic coverings on the greenhouses shook and shivered. The noise of their roofs and a harrier that was screeching piercingly as it rose through the blue sky were the only things you could hear throughout the valley.

Go ahead, after you, said Sakoiti and opened the door.

The house had two rooms of bare brick, its openings painted electric blue.

This is the kitchen, said Sakoiti and indicated a Formica table, two chairs, a cupboard, a desk covered in papers. Leaning up against a corner were a bunch of shovels and rakes, scissors hanging from a nail in the wall.

From now on, I'll keep the tools in the shed, I promise, said Sakoiti and took her into the bedroom and showed her a dark wardrobe, a double bed, some black curtains with big red flowers. He pointed to each thing and said its name.

This is the bed, he said. It's new, I bought it for you, because you were coming. These are the pillows. The blanket. It's a new mattress, the sheets are new, it's all of the best quality, he said.

He showed her the bathroom and showed her the fridge-freezer and the heater and the pots.

This is the pot. This is the pan. This is the smaller pan. They don't sell them separately. You get the whole set or nothing. Do you like them?

Yes, said Mabel.

Do you like the freezer? Nobody has a freezer here. You'll be the only one, the others just have a little ice box at the top of the fridge.

Yes, I like it, said Mabel.

And the sheets? The bathroom? Do you like the bathroom? It's a good bathroom, with ceramic fittings, of the best quality, do you like it?

Mabel nodded. She moved towards the window and looked at the greenhouses, the open field, the road, the tents belonging to the other Japanese people, in the distance.

And the reservoir? she asked.

It's very close, just on the other side of the mountains.

Can you walk there?

It's a long walk, but yes. It's a nice view. You can see the wall of the dam, and the power station.

Maybe I'll go up tomorrow, said Mabel.

Tomorrow or whenever you want. You're going to like it here, said Sakoiti. You'll see, you're going to be happy, you're going to like it.

Then he pulled the curtains all the way closed.

Would you prefer it like this or with the light coming in? he asked, approaching her.

Like this is good, said Mabel.

You relax, deep breaths, just let go, said Sakoiti.

Yes, said Mabel.

Are you comfortable? Are you relaxed? You can concentrate on how it feels, I'm going to give you pleasure, said Sakoiti.

Yes, yes, I'm fine, said Mabel.

When he finished, Sakoiti lit a cigarette and stood by

the window, smoking. It was dark now outside, and the lights of the other greenhouses formed a shining garland all along the road.

You didn't relax, said Sakoiti. If you do not go deep inside yourself, you won't feel anything.

Mabel turned on the bedside lamp, found her clothes and got dressed.

Sakoiti took another drag of his cigarette.

You have to relax, he said.

Next time, I promise, said Mabel and put on her socks.

Yes, yes, you have to relax, said Sakoiti. You'll see, I'm going to treat you like a queen, you're going to like it here.

Sakoiti took Mabel to pay a courtesy call to the other greenhouses. At the first house they met a Japanese woman sitting in the sun, selecting buds. With quick hands she tore off the petals that were split or had stains. As soon as she saw them coming down the road, the woman put aside the heaps of roses and went out to welcome them. She greeted them by bowing her head and sent one of her children to get his father, to let him know that people had arrived.

Seeing Mabel, the Japanese men raised their arms and launched serious exclamations filled with oohs and aahs that sounded like shouts of amazement or of joy.

They say that they are very happy that you are my wife now, translated Sakoiti. They're congratulating us.

The Japanese kids, meanwhile, were circling around Mabel and laughing, and one, at the third plant nursery, went up to Sakoiti and whispered something into his ear.

Sakoiti let out a guffaw.

He's asking if he may touch your hair, he explained

to Mabel. Around here we are not very accustomed to seeing hair like yours.

Yes, yes, of course, said Mabel, and the boy squeezed between his fingers one of her curls while all around them everyone looked on in astonishment.

Now they all want to touch it! said Sakoiti, amused, and he made signs to the other Japanese to come on up.

Mabel sighed and said nothing.

One by one the children went up to her, and Mabel had to crouch down so they could stroke her head.

In the end, with much embarrassment, the Japanese woman also asked permission to touch her. She plunged her fingers into Mabel's hair, all the way up to her knuckles, and she released and contracted them several times, her eyes shining with surprise.

Then she withdrew her hand fast and bowed.

She says it's like rapids with dry water in them, Sakoiti translated what the woman was saying. That means it's beautiful, that it is very lovely. It's a compliment, he said.

Mabel thanked her with a smile.

The Japanese woman clasped her hands over her chest and bowed to her again.

No woman came out to receive them at the last greenhouse, the furthest from Sakoiti's house, right where the road began.

Hiroki! Hiroki! Sakoiti shouted as loud as he could. An old dog sleeping in the damp sand raised its head, looked at them a while and kept on sleeping. Alongside the house a car with no wheels sat rusting; they had covered the windshield with wire mesh, and it now served as a chicken coop.

Hiroki! Hiroki! Sakoiti shouted again, in the direction of the tent.

A Japanese boy peeked out of one of the windows of the house and looked at them with bulging eyes, the palms of his hands resting on the glass.

That's Hiroki's son, he isn't normal, Sakoiti explained to Mabel. There is something wrong with his brain.

Mabel turned towards the window. The little Japanese boy was probing the glass with his tongue.

Don't look at him, said Sakoiti. He only wants attention.

Where's his mother? asked Mabel.

She died, three or four years ago. A long illness.

At the door of the greenhouse appeared a Japanese man, very tall, with a great deal of grey hair and leathery skin. His trousers were stained with mud, and when he saw the boy in the window, he gestured to him to go away. The little Japanese boy immediately took a step backward and disappeared into the shadows inside the house.

Sakoiti bowed before the man and introduced them.

This is Hiroki. He's our oldest settler, he told Mabel. He was the first to arrive. He speaks Spanish very well. It is thanks to him we are all here.

That's right, said Hiroki.

It's good that Sakoiti has a woman now, it's high time, he said then. He came here very young and worked very hard, and he deserves this.

Sakoiti nodded, lowering his head.

I insisted he get a Japanese woman, said Hiroki, but none of them convinced him. He wanted a woman from this country. I am not so sure that this is the right decision.

There's no need for you to tell her that, Sakoiti murmured.

He says that the women from here are much more beautiful than our own, Hiroki continued without paying any attention. To me it seems they are simply different.

Mabel felt Hiroki's hard gaze fall upon her.

But what has been done is done, said Hiroki. I will not keep you further. I wish you all the best, and I hope that harmony will reside in your home, and that you will always know how to tend to each other.

Thank you, said Sakoiti and clasped his hands over his chest. I will behave in the best way, he said. I will work hard.

Yes, said Hiroki and turned and went back inside his greenhouse.

Hiroki was very happy with his wife, Sakoiti told Mabel later, as they were walking back down the road. He was the one who taught me how to treat a woman. He explained everything I needed to know, he said. I will be a good lover to you, you'll see.

Every morning Sakoiti got up when it was still completely dark, turned on the lights in the greenhouses and went around in the rows between the plants. Mabel could see his shadow from the window, lengthening over the plastic walls, coming and going on a sea of carnations, harvesting the buds that had opened.

When he finished, Sakoiti would come back to the house, pour himself a cup of steaming coffee and drink it quickly, down in one, leaning against the doorframe, the truck's engine already running outside, warming up in neutral. Then Sakoiti would load the carnations and go into the city to sell them. Mabel would stay behind watching the truck's lights getting further away along the road, only slightly diffused behind the dust sent up by the wheels.

Those first days in the house by herself, Mabel took

the opportunity to inspect the wardrobe, all the drawers, the desk heaped with papers, time deposit receipts, a cheque book from the bank and his account statements. Wrapped in tissue paper, at the bottom of a drawer, she found a dry leaf from some very large tree, but she could not think what kind of tree it was. Inside a dusty box, at the very top of the wardrobe, there were different books on learning Spanish. Mabel spread them out over the table, turning their pages one by one, reading the underlined sections, the spaces for the exercises completed in Sakoiti's careful penmanship, copying again and again the same words and phrases and practising the conjugations of the verbs. When she finished looking through them, Mabel put them back how they had been and closed the wardrobe doors on them again.

In one of the bedroom walls, facing the window, there was a small niche carved into the brick and covered with a tiny white curtain made of cloth. Inside, at the back of the niche, rested a picture of an older couple. Both were Japanese and wearing kimonos. They were kneeling, with their hands in their laps, palms up. The woman's hair was white; the man looked older, but his moustache was still dark, without any grey in it.

In front of the photo there was a blue ceramic bowl, with half a centimetre of water. Even though Mabel never saw Sakoiti go up to the niche, let alone raise the curtain, some mornings she found a carnation proppe against the bowl when she awoke. Other mornings, a very green feather, or a dry and twisted branch, or a little pile of seeds, or a quartz stone.

Sometimes, Mabel lifted the curtain and inside the niche there was only the picture, with the empty bowl upside down.

Sakoiti would return from the market just before noon. Then Mabel would spread out the tablecloth over the table and serve lunch. Before sitting down, Sakoiti would wash his hands and face in the kitchen sink. Some days, as he was drying himself, he would make a comment about the price of the flowers and his sales, if they had been very good, if they had been very bad. Mabel, from time to time, would remind him to add a certain cleaning product to his shopping list. They almost always ate in silence. When they had finished, Sakoiti would unload his supermarket purchases from the truck and put them away in the cupboard. Mabel would wash the dishes. Sometimes she would stop, as if lost, with her forearms covered in suds and a ladle in her hand, looking out the window, her eyes mixing up the sun-bleached mountains with the trembling where her face was reflected.

The water from the tap would run over the dirty pots. Sakoiti would find a dishcloth and start to dry off the plates.

Are you alright? Is there something wrong? he would ask her.

Yes, yes, I'm fine, Mabel would say and go on washing.

What are you thinking so hard about?

Nothing, I'm not thinking about anything.

Do you miss it?

What do you mean?

The pine forest, the cabin.

No, said Mabel.

Then what's wrong?

Nothing. I'm fine.

Every other weekend, Sakoiti drove Mabel to the rest home. He stayed outside in the truck, and Mabel and old Wutrich took a walk around the porch that went the whole perimeter of the building and then sat a while looking out at the lawn. Then they went back to his room, and Mabel made sure the bathroom was clean and that they had changed his sheets.

Do you remember that loose floorboard in the cabin, right in front of the stove? said Wutrich. The other day I was thinking about it. I don't know why. How many years was it like that? Both of us had learned to go around it, even in the dark we never tripped over it. Last night I was lying here, and I just started thinking about that board, and the floor, and that I should have replaced it, and I was trying to remember what I would have been doing, what I could have been so busy with that I never had time to fix it.

It was fine like that, Mabel said then. There wasn't any need to replace it.

Do you remember everything I used to do there in the pines? said Wutrich then. Moving saplings, trimming branches, weeding in the winter, keeping the fires in check during the summer.

Mabel was looking at her nails, taking a little piece of skin in her teeth and biting it.

Do you remember the time those hunters got in close to the stream and started a fire? Wutrich was saying. It was a good thing you spotted the smoke. We put it out just before it started to take off, otherwise I don't know what would have happened. And do you remember the time our little brown goat got lost, and we went up to the very top to see if we could find her, and we got caught after dark up there by the ridge?

I remember, I was little then, said Mabel.

Do you remember when we were on the way to sell squash in town, and the bag broke on us, and the squash popped out and rolled down, right at Stucky's slope, and you ran to grab them, and I shouted out to you, watch out for the edge, Mabel, watch out for the edge?

Mabel was smiling.

Just think of all the things we've done together, the two of us, old Wutrich said then, and he patted Mabel on the shoulder.

Just think of all the things we've done together, he said again, and then fell quiet.

Was it with you that we planted the pines? he asked after a while.

No, Dad.

We'd extend a wire, and wherever the marker fell, we'd dig a little hole, and that would be where the pine would go. If it hit stone or a very steep slope we'd skip it and go on, keeping to a straight line. That wasn't with you?

No, Dad. That was a long time before I was born.

Old Wutrich nodded and stared at the white streaks in the linoleum on the floor.

Four hundred and fifty thousand pines, he said. We transported them on horseback. And then, all these years.

Alright, Dad, Mabel said. Don't think about that. Have you gone into the pool? Have you seen any films in the cinema, at least?

I went one time, but you couldn't hear anything. Then I went again, and they had cancelled it.

What about the pool?

Not yet.

Why?

Old Wutrich shrugged.

All those pines up there, he said, growing so slowly you wouldn't even notice it.

Sakoiti was afraid that Mabel would get bored, so he asked some of the Japanese women to go and keep her company a couple of times a week. Every Tuesday and Friday afternoon, the women would arrive in single file, walking along the dry bed of the river. They would greet Mabel with a little bow, take off their coats and sit down around the kitchen table, to embroider in their little taborets, to mend tears or darn socks.

Mabel would serve them an entire packet of biscuits on a plate, and they would reach out to take them one by one.

Mabel sat with them and watched them work. Sometimes, if they caught each other's eyes while reaching for a cookie, they would exchange a shy smile or a small gesture, as of recognition. Then, the Japanese women would put their heads back down and keep on sewing.

When the cookies on the plate ran out, the women would rise, put on their jackets, and say goodbye, taking another little bow.

Did the women come to keep you company? Did you serve them the biscuits? Did they eat them? Sakoiti would ask at night, when he would come back from the greenhouse.

Yes, they came.

Did you have a good time? Did they like the biscuits?

Yes, yes.

Should I buy more at the supermarket, or are there still some left?

There are four packets still in the cupboard, you don't have to get more yet.

Great, that's great, I'm very glad, Sakoiti would say and turn on the shower and wait for the water to get hot.

With a brush he would scrub out the black dirt that remained under his nails; lathering himself up painstakingly, he would wash his face, his hair, his armpits and behind his ears. The hot steam escaped from the bathroom through the slightly open door and filled the room with the smell of soap and chamomile shampoo. Sakoiti returned to the bedroom whistling, with a towel around his waist and a trail of little droplets that trembled on his very pale, very smooth skin.

Now you have to relax, he would say. Let's see if you can manage it today. Remember how I taught you, breathe deeply, he would say.

Let's see, come on, relax.

The clear skies of autumn made way for a grey winter and low-slung clouds. As the days became shorter and shorter, the cold firmed up its hold over the valley where the plant nurseries were kept.

In the mornings, the air inside the house was so freezing that sometimes, when she had finished cleaning up, Mabel would run over to the tents and let the hot fumes of the greenhouses crush her like a pillow over her chest. She would take off her jacket, take off her sweater, and be barefoot and feel the humidity of the carnations clinging to her cheeks and hair, running down her back, her neck, in between her skin and the fabric. The humidity formed condensation on the insides of the walls, clouding the plastic and making it opaque. From the ground rose a metallic smell, a little synthetic, the smell of phosphorous and urea. Floating in that chemical and ashen light, Mabel would walk among the rows of carnations. Droplets of sap would glisten on the stems that Sakoiti had cut that morning and on the buds that were still growing, striving upwards, their petals trying hard to emerge and be harvested the next morning. Mabel saw them flowering, and, sometimes, she would pluck one and crush it in the palm of her hand and throw it down on the ground.

Then she would go back to the freezing house, make the bed, do the laundry, polish the colander, the pans, the cutlery, chop onions, make lunch.

What would happen to the carnations if they didn't have the tents? she asked Sakoiti one afternoon.

He was looking through his account books, hunched over his desk. They would get frostbite, he said. They would get spindly and yellowed, and then they would die.

Mabel nodded and went back to looking out the window.

Sakoiti stretched, making his vertebrae crack, then continued with his additions and subtractions.

When it got dark outside, and he stood to turn on the light, Mabel was still standing there leaning her forehead against the glass, looking outside.

You are bored, said Sakoiti.

I'm a little tired.

Do you not feel well? Are you sick?

I'm fine, there's nothing wrong, said Mabel.

Sakoiti nodded.

What did you do there?

There where?

What did you do with your time? Back in the pine forest?

Same as here.

Didn't you get bored?

I'm not bored here, either. I'm fine.

How did you fill the hours?

I cooked, I cleaned. I don't know, same as here.

And you didn't get bored.

No, no, like I said, I'm fine.

Would you like to take a walk maybe? We could go up and see the reservoir, in the end you never went up there.

Maybe another day, not right now.

Do you want me to buy you a chicken?

No, good God, what a nuisance. What would I want a chicken for?

In the pines you had chickens...

No, no, no. Don't even think of buying me a chicken, I'm serious.

Well, then?

I don't need anything, I'm fine.

One day old Wutrich was in his bed, with the remote control in his hand and the TV turned off, when a nurse came in and said that someone had come looking for him.

Who came looking for me? asked Wutrich.

A man.

A Japanese man?

No, normal.

Old Wutrich nodded.

The visitors' room had white walls and armchairs arranged in pairs. Outlined against the diffuse clarity of the curtains, a man was waiting looking out at the lawn. It took Wutrich a minute to recognise him. Then he brought his hand to his heart.

What's happened? he asked. Is it Mabel? Has something happened to Mabel?

Moro Scarafia looked at him perplexed.

Not that I know of, he said. I haven't seen her again since that day.

What are you doing here? Wutrich asked him immediately.

Then Moro Scarafia understood.

I'm not here for professional reasons, he said smiling. I'm sorry if I scared you, I just wanted to visit you. See how you were doing.

Wutrich squinted, not believing him.

It's me, Moro.

Yes, I know, said Wutrich. So Mabel is fine? No bad news?

Everything is fine, said Moro Scarafia.

Old Wutrich dropped into one of the armchairs and let out a sigh of relief. Almost immediately, the sigh turned into a coughing fit.

You came all the way here, he said when he'd recovered.

I had heard this was the best of the best, but I wasn't fully convinced, said Moro Scarafia.

Wutrich nodded.

How's everything going in town? Any news?

Same old, same old.

No one died?

Just La Alda.

Who?

La Alda Pidino, tall, big hips, Carazo's Señora's sister. It had been years since she last left the house.

Oh, I know the one, said Wutrich. We were in the same class in school.

Moro Scarafia sat down beside him in an armchair.

Cortenga died, too, but I think you were still around when that happened. The funny thing was that when we got to the cemetery I realised I had forgotten the key to the chapel. In thirty years, that's the first time that that's happened. I had to run back to get it.

Old Wutrich said nothing.

What about the pines? How are the pines holding up? he asked after a while.

They're just about done, said Moro.

Old Wutrich sighed and looked at his hands.

This is such a nice place, said Moro Scarafia.

Yes, it's nice.

And Mabel?

Mabel is Mabel.

Moro Scarafía scratched his beard.

She's doing well?

Yes, she's well.

Is she still with the Japanese fellow?

How do you know she's with a Japanese fellow?

That's what they've been saying, you know how people are.

Yes, said Wutrich.

I keep thinking about that one time, said Moro Scarafía then.

What one time?

The time you came to my house, that morning.

Oh, sure.

Some days I still think about it, said Moro Scarafía. Obviously I couldn't have bought you all this.

Old Wutrich looked at the armchairs, the curtains, the wallpaper.

Anyway, what can you do, said Moro Scarafía.

Sure, exactly, said Wutrich, and he yawned and pressed his palms against his eyelids.

Later he told Mabel about it, the next weekend, when she went to visit him.

Moro Scarafía? Here? she said.

You got it, said old Wutrich.

Mabel had spent the past few weeks knitting him a sweater, and now she wanted old Wutrich to try it on. It was a light blue pullover, with cuffs and two patterned bands across the belly in light brown. Sakoiti had bought her the wool.

For me? asked Wutrich, taking it by the shoulders.

I made the neck the way you like it, so it won't scratch you, said Mabel as she helped him put it on. She adjusted the shoulders and sleeves for him.

Fits like a glove, said old Wutrich.

Tight at the armpit?

No, not at all.

Sleeves are a little long.

No, no, said Wutrich, it's great. I'll roll it up a little
and it'll work just fine.

I don't know what I was thinking, they're too long,
said Mabel.

Don't you worry, I'll ask the nurses to wash it, and
I'm sure it will shrink.

So what did Moro Scarafia want that he came all this
way? asked Mabel.

Old Wutrich shrugged.

He said he didn't have too much to do and that he
wanted to take advantage of the price of gas being down.
He asked after you, I told him you were fine.

Mabel nodded.

I'll see about knitting you another one, she said. I'll
just have to ask the Japanese fellow to buy me some more
wool. What colour would you like?

Any colour, said old Wutrich. Or green, ask him to
get you green.

Mabel went up along the path that started behind
the tents, she had once seen a couple of the Japanese
kids climbing around back there. It didn't even take
her twenty minutes to get to the ridge. The peaks there
weren't great sharp fingers of rock, like in the pine forest,
but rather whaleback mounds of loose, round pebbles.
The reservoir appeared in front of her, flat and metallic,
the sun glinting on the water. There were no birds in the
sky, and under the harsh light of high noon, everything
looked static and white.

Mabel's eyes travelled around the lake's edge, which towards the plain got wider. On her right she could see the wall of the dam, tiny in the distance, and, off to the side, the blocky power station. Much further out, where the lake seemed to get lost in the mist of the horizon, a dark, layered fog made up in the sky a greyish smudge against which the glass and steel domes of certain edifices stood out.

Mabel sat down on the stones and stayed staring at the city behind the fumes. The dust had dirtied her shoes, and it was sticking to the sweat over her lips, to the skin of her face and her arms. She shielded her eyes with her hand and tried to make out more details: the shine of an antenna, a chimney, the bell tower of some church.

A silvery plane came up out of somewhere behind the lake, close to the city, and rose through the blue sky. Two little red lights flickered on its wings, the sun gleaming over its metallic side. The plane veered, showing its white belly, and moved away towards the horizon. Once she could no longer make it out in the brightness of the sky, Mabel got up and started heading back down again.

At her feet she could see Sakoiti's tents and the pile where he threw the ends of the stalks, the discarded leaves, the plants that had dried out already. Seen from above, the greenhouses seemed to be crushed against the ground, wide and grey like toads. Further, along the river, there were the tents of the other Japanese people, and after that mere plains.

Sakoiti was waiting for her with the table set.

Is that the city that's on the other side? asked Mabel.

Yes, said Sakoiti. You can see it on a clear day, or at night, when they turn on the lights.

Mabel cut a piece of bread and brought it to her mouth. She chewed in silence.

Are you OK? Sakoiti asked her.

Yes, yes.

I want you to be OK, said Sakoiti. For both of us to be OK. For us to be happy.

Mabel swallowed.

Don't you worry, she said.

He knew where the guard posts were and at what times the motorcycle patrolled around the lawn, so old Wutrich had no trouble running away. He jumped the earthen wall at the back, the furthest away, and walked quite a while crossing fields, until he found an asphalt road. He sat down under a tree and stayed there, not moving, just waiting. When he saw a truck coming up, he went out to the intersection and motioned with his arm.

Where are you headed, friend? the trucker asked him.

That way, said old Wutrich, pointing ahead.

The trucker was driving with the window down and his elbow resting on the frame. He asked a couple of questions, old Wutrich offered to brew him mates and the trucker said there was no need. The road had already turned into a wide highway. On either side, you could already see little shrub-like trees, yellow scrubland, sheep, fences. Then, timidly, green grass, the occasional cow.

I really have to piss, said old Wutrich, and they pulled over.

Wutrich pissed watching the wind flutter over some lowland where somebody had sown alfalfa.

The trucker took the opportunity to check the tyre pressure.

What are you carrying? old Wutrich asked him.

I work for the quarry, I've just got sand, said the trucker.

Old Wutrich got back in the truck, and they headed off again.

On the other side of the window appeared fallow pastures, rectangles of very green wheat, from time to time the lash of a dirt road that interrupted the fence and went into the fields. And sort of sprinkled out around the grid of the pastureland, some houses with their little hill of trees for firewood, their mill, their tall eucalyptus.

Little by little it was getting dark, the highway flanked by the horizon to one side and the railroad embankment to the other. Before going all the way down, the sun pierced the cabin with its longest rays and sketched the shadow of the truck over the slope of the tracks: a black rectangle bursting over the orange weeds.

We'll have to stop for something to eat, said the trucker when the sun had fully gone.

The parrilla they went to stood next to a petrol station, by an intersection, just some eaves, an awning, and some tables made of boards with benches. Behind, under the dark murmur of some eucalyptus, four or five parked trucks.

Old Wutrich gnawed until the last string of meat stuck to the bone and had to say he was sorry, he didn't have any money. The trucker took out a couple of bills from his pocket and paid for both of them. Then he asked him again where he was going.

To the pines, said old Wutrich. I'm the one that planted them.

The trucker looked at him, not understanding.

What pines?

To the pines, old Wutrich repeated. That's where I live.

But there aren't any pines this way, said the trucker. Why didn't you say anything? You've been going in the opposite direction!

That's alright, said old Wutrich. I'm not in any hurry, there is time.

143

Another trucker, who was eating at the same table, was heading for those parts, and they quickly agreed that he would take over delivering the old man. He was younger and skinnier than the first trucker, and the cabin of his truck smelled of tobacco and wet leather.

What are you carrying? old Wutrich asked him.

Nothing right now, said the trucker. They'll be waiting on me in the morning to load the sorghum, on the other side of the mountains.

In the rearview mirror, the petrol station was already no more than a flash underpinning the night; the parrilla's sign a last lantern in the middle of the darkness and the countryside. The trucker took out a cigarette and lit it, took a long drag, the green light of the control panel dyeing his face. Outside, the white line blinked silently down the middle of the road. Old Wutrich leaned the nape of his neck back on the headrest and closed his eyes.

I'm going to rest a little while, he said.

The trucker told him to sleep as long as he wanted, since they wouldn't make it to the pines until the following day.

I'm the one that planted them, did you know that? said Wutrich. We'd extend the wire, we'd put red markers on it, and wherever a marker went in, we'd plant.

How long ago was all that? asked the trucker.

Old Wutrich hesitated.

Weren't you there? Don't you remember? he asked him.

No, Grandpa, said the trucker and smiled at him. The first time I went by, the pines were tall already.

Yes, said old Wutrich. You can see them from far away.

You sleep a while, said the trucker.

Wasn't it with you that we planted them? old Wutrich insisted. They were nicely sized then. We carried them up on horseback.

You sleep, Grandpa, get some rest, it'll do you good, said the trucker and rolled the window down ever so slightly, to let in a little air.

When he woke up, night was already dissolving into light blue, and outside there were mountains.

We'll be there soon, the trucker told him. If you want to get some mate started, the thermos is right there.

The highway went up a steep slope, and the truck coughed out smoke through the exhaust pipe. They climbed up slowly. To one side there was a precipice. Some loose stones had rolled down the mountainside and scattered across the asphalt. Further up there was a cloud stuck at the peaks awaiting them. They were submerged in it for a while, the grey, opaque humidity dissolving into drops against the windshield. Outside all you could see was boulders, the roadside ditch filled with slabs obscured by water. Until after a curve the downward slope appeared, and the truck tilted and started to descend.

There you go, said the trucker when they came down out of the clouds. He was gesturing toward some dark, vast splotches, rectangular patches over the mountain.

There you go, he said, the pine forest.

Old Wutrich smiled.

Yes, he said. The pine forest.

The trucker left him in a clearing, halfway in. In the clearing there was a goat tied to a tree, and an expanse of rocky ground. The pines shimmered on the slope ahead, past a ravine.

It's around here, I know where I am now, said old Wutrich. This must be the old road, on the other side of the town. Once I get to the crossing, I'll be almost there.

Are you sure, old man?

Yes, yes, these are the newer pines, it was some doctors from Córdoba who had these planted. The ones I was talking about are on the other side.

Old Wutrich got out and waved with his hand held high. Then, he stayed a while petting the goat's head while the truck went back up along the highway, going faster. The goat had eaten the lower branches of the tree and with her teeth she'd taken off the bark, exposing the white wood to the air. Old Wutrich scratched her behind the ears, and the goat just shook her head, as if to shoo him off.

On the hill ahead, the pine forest swayed in the breeze, its greenness lightening beneath the high sun. Old Wutrich found a stick to use as a cane and felt around on the ground, which sloped downhill. The goat stuck her neck out and let out a bleat, as if calling him, but old Wutrich paid no mind. The grass reached up to his knees, and the ground was firm and not too steep. He just had to get down to the bottom of the ravine and climb back up the slope ahead.

Off we go, it won't be long, he said to himself and started to head down, surrounded by the rustling of insects and birds.

It took him more than an hour to get to the bottom of the ravine. Along the deepest part a stream had run once, but now it was dry. Nearby grew a young and solitary pine, born of seeds the wind had brought. Its branches extended upwards, forming a cone of raised sections. The tip of the tree trembled like the flame of a candle, at the very top. Old Wutrich sat down on a rock and just watched it a while. He ran his handkerchief over the back of his neck, over his face, he cleaned off his forehead with the sleeve of his sweater. Then, he clung to the dry weeds to climb up towards the edge of the ravine.

The edge of the pine grove sketched a straight line over the mountain, a green wall, protected by three strands of rusted wire. At the base of the wall of pines, old Wutrich raised his head and looked up, to see the branches outlined against the cloudless sky.

I'm here, he said. I'm back, he said and took two steps. He took a deep breath, broadening his chest.

I'm back now, he said and plunged into the coolness of the growing pine forest, shadowy and citrusy and dusty.

A tapestry of dried needles covered the ground as far as the eye could see. Above, the wind licked the surface of the pine forest, but its gusts didn't manage to pierce the interwoven crowns, so that soon old Wutrich was surrounded by silence. Around him the steely trunks of the pines overlapped to block any glimmer in the distance.

That way, that direction. Straight ahead there's the stream, and past the stream, the path that leads to the town, said old Wutrich and set off.

He moved forward slowly, feeling around with the stick. Sometimes a log would make a slow scraping sound behind him, sometimes a bird surprised would flap between the branches. On some slopes the layer of pine needles was so thick that, when he stepped on it, the needles slid all over each other, as if they were coated in wax.

Nice and slow, there's no hurry, old Wutrich said then.

He had tied his jumper around his shoulders, and his shirt was darkening with sweat. It ran down his temples, over his forehead, made his eyes smart, permeated his face. He could feel the effort beating in his neck, thickening the blue veins in his arms, heaving in his chest. He was thirsty. He had been walking for hours among the pines and had not come across any springs or streams again. Just the pine forest, almost always identical to itself, spreading over hills and sloping expanses.

Where was the town? When had those doctors had so many pines planted? Thirst made his throat feel dry, his breath rough. He looked back: his steps had barely left any trace in the layer of pine needles. The sides of the black stones that appeared between the roots looked to him to be the same as the ones he had passed a while ago. He was tired, his tiredness was confusing him, he needed to stop and recuperate. He leaned back against the trunk of a pine tree and let himself drop, taking down with him a whole layer of loose bark. The gnarled roots scraped his shoulders and drove into the nape of his neck, but old Wutrich could no longer move and just stayed there, lying very still at the foot of the tree.

It was coming up to evening, and blue shadows were creeping over the forest. The sweat in his shirt cooled until it was freezing. Old Wutrich covered his chest with the sweater, crossed his arms. His tongue was swollen, and his mouth was very dry. His whole body was shivering. He wanted to close his mouth and couldn't. His own teeth felt strange, like bone fingers or blocks of wood embedded in his gums. His head fell to one side and, centimetres from his pupils, he saw the needles of the pines rising like spear crests. Around him he thought he could hear the bark of the pines splitting, the concentric rings pushing out the wood from inside, those rings that were imperceptible, tenacious, all the time.

It's around here somewhere, he said to himself then, in infinite exhaustion.

What's going to happen now? Sakoiti asked her in the truck.

That morning, early, they had been awakened by a policeman who had gone to the valley to let them know. They had found old Wutrich dead at the base of a pine tree, in a forest in the mountains, over a thousand kilometres from town. Nobody knew what he was doing there or how he had reached it. They identified him because he had the card from the nursing home in his pocket.

What's going to happen with what? said Mabel.

With us.

I don't know.

I'll give you all the money you want, said Sakoiti, without taking his eyes off the road. So you won't leave, so you will stay with me, he said. I'll give you whatever you want. You have seen the accounts, you know carnations make money. I'll give you whatever you ask for, but please don't go. Please, don't leave me.

Mabel looked out at the landscape through the window. The flat plain, without trees, just stones and straw, salt welts, eddies, loose soil.

Please, Sakoiti insisted.

Mabel didn't say anything.

Are you going to leave me? asked Sakoiti.

I couldn't say, said Mabel.

Moro Scarafia laid the casket where he always put them, against the back wall, between two electric altar candles, in front of the crucifix. He brought out from storage a kneeler with the base covered in red velvet, just in case Mabel wanted to kneel down before her father, and he polished the bronze fittings until they had a shine they hadn't had in years. Sakoiti had cut twenty bunches of white carnations, and he arranged them around the base of the casket, forming a kind of wave of foam that widened as it went forward. In order to accommodate all of the carnations, Moro had to move the kneeler and put the two altar candles up against the wall.

He was pretty swollen, so I decided to do it closed, he told them.

Mabel nodded.

You sure it was him? she asked.

Yes.

Sure?

Yes, yes.

Then Sakoiti squatted back down and arranged the flowers a little better, so that all of the petals would be on display, to give the feeling that it was the carnations that were holding up the coffin.

Standing next to Mabel, Moro Scarafia adjusted the knot of his tie.

Would you like us to pray? he asked.

No, thank you, she said.

At dawn, while Sakoiti was sleeping in one of the armchairs, and only a few of the churchwomen were still there beside the coffin, Mabel went out onto the pavement to get some air. The night was starry and a little cool. The crescent moon lit up the stripped mountains. Along the slopes, the stumps of the pines were no more than a scattering of dots barely unstuck from the ground. Moro Scarafia was smoking leaning against the little wall.

They logged it all, Mable said to him, signalling up in the hills.

Down to the last pine.

Yes, said Mabel and sat down next to him.

Do you want to see the cabin, how it looks now? I

can take you tomorrow, after the burial.

No. No need.

Moro Scarafia took another drag of his cigarette.

The Japanese smokes, too, he said.

Yes, said Mabel. Almost a pack a day.

Moro Scarafia nodded.

A cat crossed the street, crouching over the asphalt.

Are you sad? asked Moro Scarafia.

Mabel shrugged.

I don't know, she said. At some point it had to happen, and, in the end, his going was for the best. He wouldn't have been able to handle seeing all this.

Moro Scarafia turned to her.

And what are you going to do now? he asked her.

I don't know, said Mabel.

If you want to come back into town and need a place to stay, said Moro Scarafia. I still regret what I did that morning, when the two of you came looking for me.

Mabel smiled.

Do you want to kiss me? she asked him.

Here? Now? said Moro Scarafia.

Yes, said Mabel. Or we can go behind that wall there. Marzo's widow must be sleeping, she won't hear a thing.

Moro Scarafia dropped his cigarette and stamped it out with his foot.

Alright, sure, he said. Let's go.

They buried old Wutrich the following morning, in the cemetery that faced the stream, in the full light of the sun, on the lowest part of the hill. The priest led a prayer for the dead, with Moro Scarafia standing at his side, tall, in black and circumspect. Kovach and the head of the power station were there, and everyone from Bronzino's place. Most of them had only gone to see the Japanese gentleman.

They helped to lower the casket into its grave, and when the priest had finished, they walked off in silence. Moro took off his tie and jacket, folded them carefully and hung them over the top wire of the fence. Then he picked up the shovel and started to cover the casket with earth.

Mabel got into the truck and asked Sakoiti to turn on the engine.

Let's go, she said. Let's get out of this town right this instant.

Yes, said Sakoiti and started the engine.

They had already left behind the last mountains when Mabel turned to him and asked if he didn't ever miss Japan.

Sakoiti took a while to answer.

Yes, sometimes, he said at last.

Why did you come? What was your life like there?

My parents sent me. They always tended crops, but they didn't own anything and never could have. They saved up for many years so I could travel. With that money I bought the land from Hiroki and my first greenhouse.

They're the ones in the picture, in the wall, aren't they? said Mabel.

Yes, those are my parents.

Did they pass away?

Yes, said Sakoiti. Some time ago.

And do you like it here? asked Mabel. Are you happy?

Yes, I like it, said Sakoiti. I never would have been able to have anything like this back there.

Mabel nodded. Then she moved closer to him, in her seat in the truck.

Do you love me? she asked him.

Very much, said Sakoiti.

Will you always love me?

I hope so, if you'll let me.

Mabel smiled, not looking at him.

The windshield of the truck cut through the icy wind. Outside, the plain's minimal grass bent down under the gusts. They were close to the valley with the plant nurseries now.

Next time I'll relax, I promise, said Mabel.

Yes, said Sakoiti. We will be fine, he said. It's just a matter of time.

THE RIVER

It had begun to snow the day before, very early, before dawn, when outside the sky was dark still, and Señora Kim had not yet got out of bed. And it had snowed all day, and it had snowed all night, and now it was nearly noon, and the sky kept on releasing its relentless slow and heavy snowfall.

Snow, snow and more snow, the yard transformed into a big white field, everything levelled, everything covered. Snowflakes piling up against the window to build an impenetrable wall. So that it was as if the river no longer existed, and nor did the bridge, nor the sawmills on the other side of the river, not even the hills and the mountains. There was only snow, and more snow. Up above, the blue shadow of the storm, stirring calm.

That morning, the piano teacher's grandchildren had gone outside to play on the pavement, and Señora Kim had entertained herself by watching as they built a snowman. They compacted the snow in their hands, formed a big ball of it, slapped its sides. The piano teacher's wife was monitoring their activities from the verandah, and when they began exchanging snowball fire, she went out to retrieve them.

That's enough, she told them. Inside, come on inside now, she said, and bade them follow her into the house.

Stupid woman, muttered Señora Kim, standing by the window. When she was a child, there was nothing in the world that pleased her more than playing in the snow and making snowmen with her sister.

What's the point in getting married all over again? said Señora Kim.

She had never been particularly fond of that second wife of the piano teacher's.

The piano teacher's first wife had died a few years earlier, run over by one of the sawmill trucks. Not long after, the teacher had brought home that other woman, who was tall, big-boned, Swedish-looking, maybe Norwegian. Nobody in town knew who she was. A few thought they remembered her from one of the teacher's recitals at the school auditorium. Sitting in the back row, they said, I'm sure of it, being discreet, keeping her hair up in a kerchief.

The new wife wasn't young. She was more or less the same age as her predecessor, the same age as Señora Kim, the same age as the teacher. Her face cracked into little wrinkles, her hair she wore loose over her shoulders, dried out and brittle, an electrified grey. She wore trousers that were too big for her, men's boots, loose shirts.

What would be the point, at our age? He can barely stand on his own two legs these days, hardly moves at all, muttered Señora Kim each time she saw that woman.

That day the teacher had no students, but when the clock struck noon, he nonetheless sat down at the piano. From her kitchen Señora Kim could hear him playing, amidst the snow's muffled grazing. At first she thought that he was playing some silly song to entertain his grandkids, but then the melody unravelled into a strange scale, a little sad, a little bit haphazard, as though the teacher were paying no attention to the keys, his fingers shuttling to and fro without direction.

He's gone and locked himself inside his study so nobody will bother him, Señora Kim said then.

He can't stand his grandkids anymore, she said. He wants to be alone, and he has no idea how to get rid of that wife of his.

Señora Kim put some leftover soup on the stove, and while she was waiting for it to heat, she dialled her daughter's number.

It's been snowing here for two days, she said by way of hello. Shows no signs of stopping.

Señora Kim's daughter was named Nuri. She was a nurse, and she lived abroad, on another continent. There wasn't much of a time difference, but where Nuri was, it was summer. Señora Kim's daughter had rented a room in a flat that also overlooked a river, a flat on the fourth floor facing the street, without a lift. From her bed she could see the park on the banks of the river and, in the autumn, when the trees would lose their leaves, she could also see a bit of the water. Señora Kim knew the place from photos. They'd come in an airmailed envelope: two photos, one of the room, the other of the view from the window. Accompanied by a short letter, the handwriting hurried, the paper extremely thin. Señora Kim's daughter shared that flat with three other women, also nurses. They got along well enough, all four of them worked for the same hospital, which was nearby, they all had different shifts, were almost never home at the same time.

Sometimes, when her daughter seemed to feel like talking, Señora Kim would insist that she look for a flat of her own. You slave away up there, she told her daughter, there's no reason for you to be sharing a bathroom with other people.

Nuri would say yes, she knew, but that everything was very expensive there.

You don't get it, Mum. You have no idea what it's like here, she would say, and then she'd hang up the phone.

Señora Kim ate her soup leaning up against the doorframe, looking out at the river, or at where the river ought to have been, behind all that snow in the air. The steam from the soup fogged up the window, and Señora Kim cleaned it off with her hand. Then she washed the bowl and the spoon, dried them and put them away. The boards of the staircase creaked beneath her feet when she went up to the second floor. The thick silence of the snowfall had taken over the bedrooms, too, and in her room all that was audible was the secret swallowing of the radiators and a raspy gurgle every so often. Señora Kim's room looked out over the back of the house, and from there she could see the backyard, completely covered, a little pine curved under the weight of the snow, the dark branches of a leafless bush reaching out from the white like the fingers of a buried bony hand.

It used to be Señora Kim's husband who took care of the garden. When he was younger and going to a school run by priests, Señora Kim's husband had studied botany and gardening. He'd become such an expert on plants and at some point, not long after they'd got married, he'd even fantasised about opening up a plant nursery in town, by the highway, in the curve of the ramp.

Where'd you come up with that idea? Who do you think is going to buy flowers in a place like this? Señora Kim had told him then.

In the end, the project never quite took off, and his gardening never became anything more than just a pastime.

Señora Kim saw a man walking in the snow, down the street behind the house that ran along the garden. The man was wearing a black hat and a big puffy green jacket, and he had his hands in his pockets. The man went up to Clauster's bar, and then when he found the shutters drawn and the bar closed, he turned right around and retraced his steps.

In spring and summer, those men were always a problem. They'd sit around and drink beer on the kerb, and they'd remain there until late, yelling, laughing, fighting. Some of them would sometimes urinate on the garden. Señora Kim and her husband would hear them from their bed, both of them lying there unable to sleep.

Because of this, while he was alive, Señora Kim's husband hated Clauster with all his might. Every time a drunk would piss on his plants he would report it to the police.

They're going to destroy all of my lilies, he used to say.

Oh, Goro, cut it out, Señora Kim would scold him. Just go to sleep and leave it alone, it won't do any good to call.

Clauster has a deal with the police chief, he pays him bribes, there's no point in complaining, she would try to explain to him.

But Goro didn't care.

Officer, it's Señor Kim, he would say into the phone. The drunks are in our yard again. Just come and see what they've done. Get your vehicle out and come on over.

Now Señora Kim got along fine with Clauster. It wasn't as though they were friends, but if they passed each other on the street they'd say hello, and when Señora Kim ran out of bread or sugar, she'd go to the bar, and Clauster would sell her some.

He charged her a little more than standard, but at least she didn't have to walk the ten blocks to the supermarket.

Sometimes Clauster was having a good day, and after they had settled up he'd chat with her a while, leaning up against the counter, between the display case of cigarettes and the glasses on their trays. He'd tell her stories about his regulars, talk to her about a girlfriend he had, a car he wanted to get rid of. Señora Kim had got what she'd come for, and had paid for it, and had no reason to remain there any longer, and yet Clauster kept on talking to her, and her without any idea how to escape.

Yes, yes, oh certainly, she'd say when she could and turn around and walk out without saying goodbye.

Since her husband died, if the drunks made noise in front of the bar, Señora Kim just sat in bed and watched them. If one of them tried to urinate on her garden she'd open the window and yell at him. Even though there wasn't a single weapon in the house she'd threaten to blow their heads off with a shotgun.

At first, Señora Kim had done the impossible to

maintain the garden as her husband had left it. She weeded it and sprayed for ants and watered it each afternoon. It pained her to think of all his years of hard work going to waste, but her efforts were in vain. She didn't have green fingers, didn't know a thing about plants. By the time summer was over, the yard was nothing but misshapen, overgrown bushes, dehydrated flowers, ruined leaves. And now the snow, compacting all of it, turning it all white.

From the river blew an icy wind and a wisp of a draft whistled around the room on streaming in between the window and its frame. Señora Kim put a pillow underneath her legs, crossed her hands over her chest, and rested flat on her back in bed for a while. She thought of all those distant snows, the real snowfalls back when she was young and lived in the yellow house surrounded by pines, on the other side of the river, upriver, those great pine forests of her youth. Señora Kim closed her eyes and pretended she was still in the bed that had been hers back then, in the room she had shared with her sister, back then in the yellow house. The window on the right, the chest of drawers with the broken handle, the rickety drawers. Little pictures of saints hung up and down the hallway, but she never quite got to see them, since they were posted so high. Inside the broom closet someone had pinned up the painting of a lake in the middle of the mountains. Whenever she could, Señora Kim would sneak a candle in to look at it. The smell of kerosene and mops from the broom closet and, in the middle of the lake, a gigantic fish, arching in the air, leaping into the light of the flame. Get out of there before you set something on fire, her mother's voice would reach her from the hallway. Go outside a while, she would say, go and play with your sister.

Señora Kim nodded off for a minute and lost her

train of thought. Her memories blurred, now she was elsewhere. On top of a wooden table there was a big pile of white snow. Her husband was there, sitting at the table. He plunged his hands into the mountain of snow and took something out from inside of it. Señora Kim's husband showed her the palms of his hands. On them rested something damp and round, a ball of wet hair. Goro, is that you? Señora Kim asked him. What is that you have there? What are you trying to tell me? A gust of snow rattled the windowpane. Goro was trying to tell her something, and Señora Kim wasn't able to understand him. She opened her eyes, gazed up at the ceiling, at the nightstand and its cover, the snowflakes stuck to the window like bird shit.

Señora Kim reached over for her watch. She'd hardly slept a wink.

Outside the snow spun around in a whirlwind. The wind was making the rafters creak, barraging the exterior. Señora Kim made some coffee and poured herself a big cup.

Maybe, before he'd died, her husband had planted bulbs in the yard, and now he was wanting her to save them.

Maybe they had been forgotten underground, bulbs from years gone by, and Goro was alerting her that underneath all of that snow those bulbs were sprouting, and it was up to her to protect them, make sure the snow didn't destroy them.

Señora Kim looked outside and took a sip of coffee.

If those bulbs are down there, Goro my dear, I can tell you right now that I will not be going out under such conditions for their sake.

Next door, the piano teacher's wife went out into their garden with a shovel. She'd put on a red hat and a yellow plastic poncho, the kind they give to tourists on rainy days, on tours. The piano teacher's wife shoved the sleeves of her poncho up to her elbows, jammed the shovel into the snow and hoisted up a little heap that she discarded to one side. She kept at this for quite a while, clearing the concrete path that ran from the verandah to the street. She shovelled hard, three, four, five shovelfuls, and then she'd stop and lean against the handle and give her shoulder a little massage.

Stupid woman, no sense whatsoever in clearing the path until the storm dies down.

Maybe it wasn't a bulb, maybe it was a really big seed, brown and fuzzy, that Goro was showing me, said Señora Kim, and she brought her cup to her lips.

All those giant pines, before they had been logged. Their silhouettes against the orange dusk. All the pines at the yellow house. *Pinus elliottii, pinus tadea, pinus radiata,* her husband would have said. Goro had that habit. For every plant, every flower, every insignificant weed, he would give the scientific name out loud.

While she was little, Nuri was always wary. That's not true, Daddy! You made it up! she'd tell him. But it was all true, Goro never would have tricked her. One of the things he was proudest of in his life was his botany exam, in that school in the capital, when he was a pupil there. His teacher was a fat and ill-tempered priest, and the exam consisted in walking next to him through a big park, the most beautiful and the biggest park Goro had ever seen, and knowing the scientific name of whatever plant species the teacher pointed out.

Weeds, too? asked Nuri every time Goro would tell this story.

Weeds, too! Of course weeds, too, he'd answer. Even weeds have names, you know.

Señora Kim's husband had received nine out of ten points on this exam, thanks to which he had become a minor celebrity among his peers: in the entire history of the school, no one had ever managed to pass the botany class with more than a six or a seven.

Then, for years, for his whole life, Señora Kim's husband tried hard not to forget a single one of those scientific names. And if he came across some plant he'd never seen before and didn't know the name of, he'd run to look it up in his books and instantly memorize its full name, family, genus and species, common name, common uses.

Three boys bundled up in big black jackets came into view suddenly, moving down the street with the gusts of wind. They were carrying snow shovels, walking and using their hands to remove the snowflakes that kept sticking to their faces. When they saw the piano teacher's wife, they stopped in the middle of the street. The piano teacher's wife looked up and then went right back to her work. One of the boys came over, crossed the pavement and went up to her and said something. Although she couldn't quite hear it, Señora Kim supposed that the boy had offered to clear the path for her. The teacher's wife didn't respond to him or do anything. She kept transferring snow with her shovel as though the boy didn't exist. So the boy shrugged and went back to his friends in the middle of the street.

Stupid, stupid woman, said Señora Kim and quickly picked up her coat and covered up her hair with a shawl.

Hey! Hey! Kids! Kids! she shouted from the door.

The frozen air stung her face, a whistle of snow got in between her legs.

The boys approached.

Come back when the storm's over and you can clear my pavement, Señora Kim told them.

We can clear it right now. We don't know where we'll be later on.

How much do you want for it?

One of the boys said an amount. It wasn't much, they wouldn't be able to buy more than a couple of coffees with it, or one big bottle of beer at Clauster's bar to split between three.

That's fine, Señora Kim said, but there's no sense in doing it now. Come back later. And she closed the door.

Stupid kids, she said then, as she shook the snow off her shawl.

How are dad's plants doing? Nuri had asked her that morning over the phone. Did you cover them in time? Did you cover them so the snow wouldn't hurt them?

Señora Kim hadn't known what to answer.

Don't you worry, everything's fine, she'd said in the end.

When she had finished clearing half the path, the piano teacher's wife leaned her shovel up against one of the wooden columns and walked up to the verandah. She took off her gloves, threw back the hood of her plastic poncho. She sat there a while, in her red hat, her nose red, her hands shivering. It was snowing up and down the street, and soon snowflakes had splattered the two metres of pathway she had cleared. Inside, the teacher began playing a soft melody, which climbed up into the snow and rippled. The light in the sky had turned milky and dense, greyish. In less than an hour it would be dark, and it was still snowing.

Señora Kim went to find the telephone and dialled her sister's number.

I won't be at bingo today, she said. You shouldn't go, either.

Señora Kim's sister had married an English teacher, and she lived with him on the other side of the river, past the sawmills, close to where the yellow house had been before they'd torn it down. Her two daughters lived nearby, on the same street, but down the next block. In total, Señora Kim's sister had five grandchildren, two from her youngest daughter and three from the oldest.

Nuri said to say hello, I talked to her at lunchtime, Señora Kim told her sister. I told her how it was snowing here. It's summer there, it's hot. She's doing well.

Has she met anyone? her sister asked her.

No, no, said Señora Kim. She works all day. She doesn't have time for that kind of thing. Now she tells me they're going to promote her. She's going to keep working for the same hospital, but she'll get this new promotion. She just told me today.

Bless her, she was always so intelligent, said Señora Kim's sister. I hope she meets somebody soon.

Yes, yes, I hope so, too.

Slash pine, radiata pine, maritime pine, patula pine. The difference between casuarina and pine and cypress and cedar. The difference between cypress, spruce and juniper. Every time Señora Kim had gone to the hospital, she had found her husband murmuring species into his pillowcase. *Populus alba*, poplar. *Prunus serrulata*, cherry tree. *Zantedeschia aethiopica*, calla lily, he repeated with his eyes closed.

That's enough, Señora Kim had said. Sleep some, just get some rest.

But he kept going, going over time and again the names of flowers, special care instructions, when to plant and transplant, infallible methods to combat any pest. The whole time he was hospitalised.

Will you take care of my plants? he asked her that last day, when his voice was barely breath, and Señora Kim almost couldn't hear him.

Yes, I'll take care of them, don't worry.

Promise?

Of course I promise.

Señora Kim washed off her face in the kitchen sink and dried her hands with a tea towel.

Nonsense, she said. Nonsense. What's the point now in thinking about the past?

That was when she saw her, when she looked up, on the other side of the window.

It was just an instant, in the middle of the silence, enshrouded in a whirlwind of white snow. A naked woman, running towards the river. It was less than a second, and then there was nothing. Only the snow and the wind and an ashen light, increasingly opaque. It was as though she had awakened after nodding off at naptime. Without knowing how, Señora Kim found herself with one hand over her mouth, shaking. Next door, the teacher was still playing the piano. Sitting on the verandah, his wife was wiping off the shovel.

Señora Kim picked up the phone and dialled her neighbours' number. The teacher did not break off his melody, it was his wife who answered.

Did you see her? asked Señora Kim. Did you see her? A naked woman running towards the river.

Who's speaking? Who is this? said the piano teacher's wife.

So Señora Kim had to explain.

Why would someone do something like that? said the piano teacher's wife. There's nobody going out in this weather.

Stupid woman, said Señora Kim as she hung up the phone.

Stupid. Stupid. Stupid.

Then she looked back outside, and there were only spirals of snow, lashing snowflakes. She dialled the police.

Officer, it's Señora Kim. The house with the gables, by the river.

No, no. It's not the drunks. I'm calling about something else this time.

Once, while he was still a boy, on the first clear day after a big snowfall, Goro was in the school playground and saw the teacher walk out of the building, perfectly calm, go down to the frozen river and start to cross it. She had made it almost halfway across when the ice broke, and the teacher was left floating on a big white sheet of it. Goro and the other kids, from the shore, shouted at her to jump off, but their teacher just stayed very still, standing up, her hands holding onto her skirt. Nobody knew what had happened. We never found out, Goro had said, the few times he had told her this story. It was almost spring by then, but the current was still slow, the blocks of ice collided without a sound, Goro said that if he shut his eyes he could still see them, could still hear that silence. The teacher was wearing a grey apron, and her shoulders were heaving like she was crying. Goro and the other kids had run downriver, tried to signal to her. There was nothing we could do, said Goro, every time he remembered it. There wasn't any way to save her, he said. Just before the old bridge the sheet of ice had flipped over, and their teacher had disappeared into the water.

Goro in her siesta. Goro's hands plunging into the pile of snow, rummaging around. Goro sitting at the table, showing her his hands. All that wet hair, there on his palms.

Goro, Goro, Goro, my God! The demands you make of me! Señora Kim protested as she pried her thickest jacket off its hanger.

She put on her woollen cap and wrapped her scarf around her neck. Her feet plunged up to her knees into the compacted snow in the front yard. It was almost night now, and the snowflakes fell in hard diagonal slashes. Señora Kim couldn't even see the trees along the riverbank.

Hello? Señorita? Is there anybody out there? she shouted into the depths of the wind.

The gale roared in her ears, the end of her scarf whipping her face.

Hello? Hello? Señora Kim yelled again, surging forward in the snow.

A gust of wind ripped off her woollen cap, which vanished somersaulting, lost in the white.

The snow surrounded her in rapid swirls, the sharp curves of the snowflakes adhering to her eyelashes.

Is there anyone there? Señora Kim asked again. Now her feet were almost at the water.

Goro, please, don't you forsake me now, muttered her frozen lips.

Then suddenly the gale calmed down an instant, and Señora Kim could hear them: the sirens, coming closer, house by house.

And the voice of a woman, invisible in the storm, calling for help from the river, calling her.

Coming, dear, just a minute! cried Señora Kim into the storm.

Just stay where you are, she told her. Don't be scared, we're almost there.

ON CONVERSATION

This is the story of a word. The word is 'swell'.

Like great fictional characters, words have lives of their own, which they lead with perfect disregard for the outward impression of consistency. Federico Falco's *A Perfect Cemetery* distinguishes itself from so much other recent fiction – in any language – by the virtues and the flaws of its characters, who are tender and irascible at once. Falco gives them to us in odd, inspired, and decisive pairings: Alba Clara and Father Sampacho, Mabel and Old Wutrich, Señora Kim and Goro's ghost, Víctor Bagiardelli and Hipólito Giraudo. Every person who helps to populate this book has already made or is about to make a clear and definite mark on the world of her story, creating an environment in which dying can be funny, reality is oneiric, and a brusque sexual initiation offers access to the sublime.

When I first met Falco's characters, I was as far away from them as possible, reading *Un cementerio perfecto* in a park at a twelve-thousand-kilometre remove from Buenos Aires, where they were born. Where I was, it was the height of summer; it was the nadir of winter where they came from. Yet each of them was instantly vivid in my mind. I could also hear them, conversing with each other in the silent cinema in which things often take place inside my brain: not Spanish or English or the German that surrounded me then, but a kind of fluid protolanguage that was nonetheless clear as a bell.

It was the emotional clarity of the communication between characters in these stories that I most wanted to preserve in my translation. Aside from honouring the author's palpable love for the landscapes of his native Córdoba Province (some seven hundred kilometres northwest of Buenos Aires), and aside from recreating the stories' contours, dazzling and precise as Frank Lloyd Wright's skylit spiral path, my most pressing concern had to do with dialogue.

The debate over how to represent place in speech has raged among translators for longer than I've been alive, and it will continue to spark fervently opposing notions long after I've retired. At stake is this question: how do you take a unique and individual form and transform it into something else that is unique and individual and that in some essential way is also identical to the first form? The point of departure and the destination must match, in other words, regardless of the journey undertaken in between.

'Vernacular is both a language always in motion,' writes translator Julia Sanches, 'breathing and reinventing itself constantly, and, perhaps paradoxically, some of the most geographically and temporally anchored language a translator can hope to negotiate.' While some translators into English search for the closest systemic equivalent − Valspeak for a certain kind of beachfront youth, Appalachian English for members of insulated communities, New England dialects for characters who hark back to traditions and who may range widely when it comes to social station − others believe that to supplant a specific time and location with a different specific time and location would not only be absurd, but would also fully erase the original culture in one fell neo-colonial swoop. Such translators must invent a new lexicon and music to house it, from scratch.

The debate rages because the question at its heart isn't answerable. The fluctuating rootedness Sanches describes can't exactly be captured, or can't be captured exactly. There isn't an answer because translation isn't a system. Translation is an encounter between two human beings that takes place in words that belong to different systems. Each of these words has changed in its identity over time. It has changed what it means, it has changed how it means it, and it has likely even changed its behaviour towards other words. The word 'conversation' first referred to 'the action of living or having one's being in a place or among persons,' or, less frequently, 'conversion.' From the sixteenth to the eighteenth century, it meant sex. It strikes me as an unusually lively word, even when compared with its most peripatetic lexical counterparts.

I can't say, then, how I approach conversation in translation in general. I can only say how I've responded to the specific opportunities presented by the stories of *A Perfect Cemetery*. Take the end of 'Silvi and Her Dark Night':

¿Cómo va a volver?, preguntó Silvi cuando el avión desapareció, por completo devorado por la claridad y la distancia.

¿Y si se pierde?, preguntó Silvi. ¿Cómo va a saber que estamos acá?

Helmut sonrió. Después abrió los brazos, bien anchos.

Mirá todo esto, dijo. ¿No es hermoso?

Sí, dijo Silvi.

No, pero prestá atención. Mirá de verdad. ¿No es hermoso?

Sí, sí, dijo Silvi.

Helmut asintió, bajó la vista, se mordió los labios.
No te preocupes, dijo. Ya va a volver, dijo. Ya nos va a encontrar.

I have translated this as:

> How will it get back? asked Silvi when the plane disappeared, fully devoured by the light and the distance.
> What if it gets lost? asked Silvi. How's it going to know we're here?
> Helmut smiled. Then he opened his arms, wide.
> Take a look at all of this, he said. Isn't it swell?
> Yes, said Silvi.
> No, no, pay attention, he said. Take a good look. Isn't it swell?
> Yes, yes, said Silvi.
> Helmut nodded, looked down, pursed his lips.
> Don't you worry, he said. It'll come back, he said. It'll find us.

Each word of my translation could be a different word instead. Silvi's first question could be: How's it going to get back? Or: How will it return? How'll it come home? Is it going to come back? Will it be able to return?

The variations could go on for pages. The same is true of any line from any story because no word is reducible to any other word. Each translation transmits at least a slightly different feeling. This is what makes the translator so powerful, even if the reader is often unaware of the extent to which her fate is in the translator's hands.

But there is one word in particular that readers have noticed and have asked about, and naturally it is the word I am least amenable to changing because it is the word to which I'm most attached.

The word is swell. I have translated 'hermoso,' which means 'beautiful,' as 'swell.' Not 'pretty,' not 'lovely,' not 'nice,' not 'extraordinary.' Swell.

If there is one thing I am sure of in the whole of my version of Federico Falco's book, it is that Helmut asks his daughter to notice how swell the world is, and how swell her future in it will be. Why? For two reasons, neither of which is currently a word: homewardness and selfness.

Perhaps no English-language author is more associated with personality or its cult than Lord Byron, whose fondness for pet words is palpable throughout the more than sixteen thousand lines of his unfinished Don Juan (1819-1824). Swell comes up five times in Canto XI, when the itinerant Sevillian *Don Juan* leaves freezing Russia for Lord Byron's native London: 'His breath, he from his swelling throat untied'; 'A thorough varmint, and a real swell'; 'So prime, so swell, so nutty, and so knowing?'; 'For those whom favour or whom fortune swells'; 'There wanted but this requisite to swell/His qualities (with them) into sublime'.

The meaning of swell in my translation corresponds closest to 3, but it carries inside it the significance of 5, along with the weight of 1, 2, and 4. Meaning 3 can be found in Hart Crane, Dashiell Hammett, P.G. Wodehouse ('it's supposed to be swell for the soul'), and many writers more, but the man whose voice I heard when I was translating this grounded and celestial scene between a father and a daughter was my own dad, whose only adjective in circumstances such as these is: swell.

Federico Falco's stories possess the lightness and the sensitivity of Wisława Szymborska, the empathy of Chekhov, the perfect structures of the greatest architects of any time. They don't really resemble Lord Byron's digressive horseplay in verse except that, in both, selves are contradictory, and selves have homes they return to, if only in their minds. Homewardness and selfness are qualities that must be specific in order to be universal; combine them, and my translation of *A Perfect Cemetery*, originally written in Spanish in Buenos Aires – the place in the world that feels the most like home to me, but where I no longer live – must reflect my own origins and orientation just as it grows out of the author's Córdoba roots and yearning.

So I have intuitively recreated on the page in English what I have seen in the movie versions of these stories in my mind. Falco wrote the screenplay, but I was the director of these sweeping films, just as you have been – as every reader will be. I hear the characters as I must, informed by all the people I have known and loved in all the places I have lived. They don't all speak the way Oklahomans speak because why would they, and because all Oklahomans do not speak in the same way. They speak according to their personalities, as Falco created them and as I read them, and the translation we have created together is now its own being, likely contradictory as any individual creation must be.

A contemporary critic wrote of Don Juan that its main failing was its contradictions: 'we are never drenched & scorched at the same instant while standing in one spot.' But Silvi is a good girl who wants to lick a Mormon who reminds her of a boy whose last rites she helped administer after an accident that has shaken her faith, and in our own irreducible ways, we are all Silvi.

Every time I read 'Silvi and Her Dark Night,' or 'Forest Life,' or indeed 'A Perfect Cemetery,' I cry. Mostly with nostalgia: an original grief coupled with the wild joy of making new homes – in languages, in life, in fiction.

(Notes: Examples of 'swell' and the history of 'conversation' come from the Oxford English Dictionary. Byron's critic was Francis Cohen, whom I read in Michael Caines' 'Isn't it Byronic?', published on July 19, 2019, in the TLS.)

Jennifer Croft
September 2020

CHARCO PRESS

Director & Editor: Carolina Orloff
Director: Samuel McDowell

www.charcopress.com

A Perfect Cemetery was published on
80gsm Munken Premium Cream paper.

The text was designed using
Bembo 11.5 and ITC Galliard.

Printed in January 2021 by TJ International
Padstow, Cornwall, PL28 8RW using responsibly
sourced paper and environmentally-friendly adhesive.

MIX
Paper from
responsible sources
FSC® C013056
FSC
www.fsc.org